Bi

by

Diana Rock

Bid To Love

Colby County Series, Volume 1

Diana Rock

Published by Diana Rock, 2022.

BID TO LOVE
Copyright © 2022 by Denise M. Long
All Rights reserved.
No part of this book may be used or reproduced in any manner whatsoever including audio recording without written permission of the author and Copyright holder.
This author supports the right to free expression and values copyright protection. The scanning, uploading, and distribution of this book in any manner or medium without permission of the copyright holder is theft of the property. Thank you for supporting this author's creative work with your purchase.
FIRST EDITION
Digital IBSN: 9781736037157
Editor: Lynne Pearson, All that Editing
This is a work of fiction. Names, characters, places, and incidents either are the product of the author's imagination or are used fictitiously, and any resemblance to actual persons, living or dead, business establishments, organizations, events, locale, or weather events is entirely coincidental.

Dedication

To all Veterinarians who work so hard to heal and keep healthy our fur or feather or scale babies.

CHAPTER ONE

Hannah's eyes darted around the shopping center parking lot and down to the roadway. The asphalt shimmered in the May heat, exuding an oily smell making her nose wrinkle. Again, she looked at her cell phone. Seventeen minutes since she had called 911. Cocking her head, she listened but there was no sound of sirens and no sign of approaching police cruisers.

Turning toward the Lexus, she shaded her eyes as she peered through the lightly tinted windows. The Yorkshire Terrier was lying on the back seat panting rapidly. When their eyes met, the dog lumbered up to the door and pawed at the glass, its tongue lolling. He gave a couple of yips before settling back down on the seat.

"Hang on, little guy. They'll be here any minute," she cried. With a fire in her gut, she decided right then she was going to break into the car herself somehow and deal with the consequences later. She searched around once again, this time for an object, any object she could use to smash the car window. But there wasn't anything around. Wiping the tears from her eyes, she stared in at the dog again.

A heavy door slammed behind her, startling her. Swiveling around she saw a white panel van ten feet away with the words, "Town of Colby, Connecticut, Animal Control" emblazoned in gold lettering on the side.

Refusing to leave the side of the Lexus, she watched a tall, handsome man in a police-type uniform walk around the front of the van and approach her. His trim, lithe body moved with ease in the unhurried manner and grace of an athlete with a hint of a swagger to his step. Taking control of the scene, his dark eyes swept the area, the lips of his wide generous mouth pressed together in a grimace on his rugged face. Hannah gulped. He was too attractive to be an animal control officer. In fact, he was downright hot. More like a state trooper or county sheriff, a pure-blooded alpha male.

"Is this the vehicle with the dog inside?" he veered to the front door of the Lexus.

"Yes, he's lying down now. Can you get him out?" She pushed a stray strand of hair away from her face. His voice was smooth as maple syrup— dark amber maple syrup.

"In a minute," He cupped his eyes to look inside the windows of the Lexus. Under his breath he swore. "He's there all right." The officer reached for the door handle and pulled but it was locked.

"I already checked the doors," Hannah shifting her weight from one leg to the other, all the while glancing at the backseat of the Lexus where the dog lay. "His eyes are closed; he may be unconscious. You have to get him out."

Circling the car, the officer checked each of the car's doors, making sure none of them had been left open. He seemed to speak through clenched teeth, his jaw barely moving. "Standard protocol."

Hannah watched as he checked the car. His light brown hair fluttered gently in the breeze. "What are you waiting for? Get him out!" she snapped, wringing her hands and bouncing on the balls of her feet.

He stopped in front of her. Hannah could see his name badge this time. It said "Officer Kelly." She was going to have to remember that for her complaint to the mayor.

"Hold on. There are procedures to follow," Officer Kelly said before turning toward the gathering crowd. "Anyone here own this vehicle?"

The fire burning in Hannah's gut raged into an inferno. This officer was wasting valuable time while that poor dog suffered in unthinkable heat. She mashed her fists together and walked in tight circles beside the car, her eyes searching heaven for help.

When no one in the crowd stepped forward, he unclipped the two-way radio from his belt. "HQ. Dog spotted in the vehicle. Owner not found. Requesting officer for entry."

BID TO LOVE

The radio responded, "All officers are on other assignments at this time. Can it wait?"

Officer Kelly frowned. "Negative. Requesting permission to enter vehicle by force."

Unable to stop herself, Hannah got right in Officer Kelly's face. "Look, you have to get that dog out of that car now," she demanded as the officer's radio squawked unintelligibly.

It must have been something important because he sidestepped her while replying, "Roger that" into the radio.

Just as Hannah went to grab him by the arm to drag him to the Lexus, he fished something from his pants pocket and pressed the metal object against the lower right corner of the front passenger window. With a crack, the window blew to pieces. Hannah and the bystanders jumped back at the explosive sound.

Reaching inside, Officer Kelly unlocked and opened the door. Leaning over the front seat, he grasped the terrier by its collar and pulled it out of the car.

Cradling the panting, conscious dog, he tried to look into its mouth and eyes.

"I'm a veterinarian," Hannah said, stepping forward and reaching her arms out toward the dog. Her hazel eyes met his wary brown eyes, over the dog's head. She straightened her shoulders and stood up taller.

"Why didn't you mention that before?" He held out the pup.

"Just hold him while I check him out. Please," she said, reaching for the dog's mouth to assess his oxygenation by the color of his gums. "It wasn't important at the time." Foul doggy smell wafted up from the dog's greasy shaggy fur.

The little dog continued to pant rapidly in Officer Kelly's arms while Hannah started her assessment. As she stroked the dog's head, her fingers brushed the officer's arm, eliciting a zing up her own arm and down her spine. She cleared her throat, "Um, eyes are clear, gums pink, maybe a little tacky. Respiratory and heart rate are increased. Do you have any water?"

Officer Kelly cradled the dog securely within his arms and headed back to the van with his charge, with Hannah following. The bystanders parted, letting them through. Kelly handed the dog to her, and disappeared into the back of the air-conditioned vehicle, returning with a bottle of cold water and a bowl.

After he filled the bowl, Hannah held the little dog to it where he drank frantically. He slurped water so fast it flew in every direction, soaking Hannah's halter top and most of her denim shorts. She shivered as the cold water hit her breasts. Then flushed hot, realizing her nipples were also responding to the cold water.

"What do you think?" Officer Kelly watched the dog as it gulped down the entire bowl full of water. His eyes kept flitting from the dog to where two hard peaks punctuated her wet halter top.

Her cheeks burning, she readjusted the dog in her arms to cover her chest. "He'll be okay, I think, but he needs an air-conditioned area and some rest." She caught another whiff of the dog, quickly adding, "And a bath."

As she said this, a white police cruiser pulled up. The policeman got out of the vehicle and asked Kelly for an update on the situation. Once Officer Kelly finished, he added, "If you agree, I'd like to take him to the shelter for a few hours. His owner can pick him up there after I cite him or her for cruelty to animals."

"Why don't you keep the little tyke overnight to be sure he's okay?" Officer Whitman said before adding, "Maybe have him checked out by the town-appointed veterinarian."

"Um, that would be me," Hannah said, swaying and rocking the dog snuggled in her arms like a baby. Still panting, it was clearly more comfortable.

Both men stared at her, their mouths agape.

"I thought Doctor Cambria was the town vet," Officer Whitman said looking from Kelly to Hannah and back again. "Doesn't that take a vote or something to change it?"

"Doctor Cambria had a stroke last night. He's in the hospital. I'm his new associate veterinarian, so I'll be taking over for him at the clinic and subbing as town vet." Hannah eyes hardened, meeting their stares. Obviously, these guys didn't get the morning memo from the vet's office yet. Or they just didn't bother reading it.

The clatter of high-heeled shoes on asphalt dragged their attention to the approaching well-dressed woman pushing a loaded shopping cart. Reaching the Lexus, she stopped beside the threesome, cooing to the dog and thrusting out her arms, expecting the dog to be surrendered to her custody. Hannah kept a tight hold on the dog.

In an irritating, high-pitched voice, the woman inquired, "How did my Shnookums get out of the car? Isn't it wonderful these brave officers were able to save you!" The dog showed no interest in its owner.

"Ma'am, is this your dog and your vehicle?" Officer Whitman inquired.

The woman looked past the officer to the Lexus. Her eyes widened as she noticed the shattered front passenger window, shards of broken glass scattered on the asphalt around the door.

"Oh, my heavens! Why, yes! Did someone break into my car to steal my precious baby?" she exclaimed. Her hand flew to cover her heart.

Officer Whitman put his hands on his hip and stood taller. "No Ma'am, we broke into your car to save your precious baby from being killed by the heat."

"What? I was only gone a few minutes, Officer. He was perfectly safe!" She laid her hand on his forearm. He shook her off with a growl.

Animal Control Officer Kelly looked at his watch as he stepped forward, handing the woman a ticket. "By my estimation, you've been gone at least forty-seven minutes. Here's your misdemeanor citation for animal abuse, cruelty, and neglect. Your court date is listed on the ticket. Your dog is being transported to the town veterinarian where he will undergo a complete physical examination, at your expense. You will receive a phone call notifying you when you will be able to pick up your dog."

He turned his back on the woman who promptly began arguing with Officer Whitman.

Reaching Hannah, Officer Kelly took the dog out of her hands. He placed the dog in a crate for transportation before turning toward her.

"So, you're the new vet?" His gaze swept her up and down, his lips pressed hard together. So hard they were almost invisible.

Hannah blushed. She crossed her arms over her waterlogged halter top to hide the wet tee-shirt effect. "Yes. That's me. Doctor Hannah Woodbridge." She held out her right hand.

Officer Kelly ignored it. Hannah's back teeth ground together.

Pulling a set of keys from his front pants pocket, Officer Kelly said, "I'll deliver the dog to the vet office." Hannah noticed he tried to avert his eyes from her chest even with her arms over it. He turned to walk back to the van.

Raising her voice to his back, "I'll call the clinic and let them know you're coming." Hannah looked down at her outfit. So much for that desperately needed shopping trip. Glancing at her watch she tried to estimate how long it would take for her clothes to dry. *Can I wait it out and then shop for what I need for the apartment?* In the background, Hannah could hear the woman arguing with Officer Whitman about the condition of her car, her precious baby forgotten. Shaking her head, shoulders slumping, Hannah headed back to her old Corolla. The morning light from her new apartment's bedroom window would be waking her up for a little while longer.

Later that night, the dog's rescue replayed in her mind. A creeping feeling of embarrassment settled over her. She had not held her composure well in the beginning. After all the training she had been through about maintaining emotional distance, she had not remained as calm as she could have done. Calm like Officer Kelly. He'd managed to keep his professionalism about him, but then, he was on duty and she was not. Hannah closed her eyes as she settled supine on the bed. Officer Kelly's dark brown eyes sprang up in her mind. She snapped her eyes open again and shifted onto her left side. "None of that," she whispered to the walls. "He's one complication you don't need. And you certainly don't need all that testosterone in your life."

As she fell asleep, her last thoughts were of her childhood dog, Blackie, and her pledge to never see another animal die an unnecessary death.

CHAPTER TWO

Andrew's teeth clenched. *What a way to start a Monday morning.* He steered the ACO van into the dirt parking lot of the vet clinic. The full parking lot told him three things. A, Doctor Cambria's practice was still going strong; B, he would probably have to wait to get the pup from yesterday's hot car rescue since he didn't have an appointment; and C, more irritatingly, he would have to park in the very back of the building and walk around to the front door in the stifling heat.

The simple white Cape with the gray shingled roof appeared dwarfed on its large grassy two-acre plot and dirt parking lot. A gray painted ramp led up from the parking lot to the front door, as much for the older owners as the older patients. The only sign sat near the entrance to the parking lot, announcing in big green letters "Colby County Veterinary Clinic."

Puffs of dirt wafted in the wake of his footsteps as he crossed the bone dry, unpaved parking area to the ramp and up to the front door. Opening the door from the alcove into the waiting area, a blast of frigid air struck his face like a slap. Behind a reception desk, Alissa Granger gave him a wave as she continued talking into the phone nestled against her cheek. Rather than sit, Andrew stood at the reception desk, quietly checking his own phone while waiting for Alissa to finish her call. When she did, she turned her bright, big, toothy smile toward Andrew and said, "Welcome, Officer Kelly. What can we do for you today? Need an appointment?"

Did she just bat her eyelashes at me? The level of heat along the collar of his shirt rose with the unease in his gut. "Ah, no — well — no. I'm here to pick up the dog brought in yesterday after the hot car rescue."

"Oh, that poor, little thing!" She dropped her voice to a whisper and leaned over the reception desk while crooking her index finger for Andrew to come closer. "Do you know that dog's owner was here already this morning trying to get him. We almost had to call the police just to get her to leave! Threatened us with all kinds of unpleasant things. Downright mean." She stepped back, fluttered her eyelashes, and gave him a brilliant smile. "You know what I'm saying?"

Andrew knew all about it. He too had put up with her shenanigans this morning. Bright and early at eight in the morning, she had been on his office door step demanding her dog back. Sounded like she had come here from his office when he told her the dog hadn't been released from the vet clinic yet.

Coughing lightly into his fist he hid his smile. "Yes, I know exactly what you mean."

"Do you want to just pick up the dog, or do you need to see Doctor Woodbridge?" She asked.

His heart rate picked up at the thought of seeing her again. "Is there any chance I can get in to see the doc and take the dog back to the shelter? Without having to wait too long? I'm expecting his mama will be looking for him again about noon."

Alissa sat back down and studied the computer screen on the center of her desk. "Hmm, all the rooms are taken." She smiled back at him, her eyes glazing over as she dropped her chin in her palm, her elbow resting on the desktop. "Say, whatever happened with that addition to the shelter you and Doc were talking about?"

Andrew rubbed the nape of his neck. "The addition?" He stared at her blankly a few seconds, then his eyes brightened. "You mean the new holding section for reptiles and other small critters?"

She sat up straighter as a woman walked out the door to the inner sanctum cradling a Shih Tzu and left the building. "Yeah, that's it." Her fingers flew on the computer keyboard.

"Nothing. No funding in the town budget." His shoulders slumped.

"That's too bad. There's a room empty now. You go wait in room four." She scribbled something down on a sticky note, folded it, and handed it to him. "I'll let the doctor know you're here." Alissa gave him a wink before he stuffed the note in his pocket and walked away down the corridor.

He entered the small exam room labeled *4 and sat down in one of the vinyl and chrome chairs set by the window. Outside, he could see the clinic sign. He shook his head, lips tight. The sign gave the impression this was the only veterinary clinic in the county. While he supposed that might have been the case when Doc Cambria first opened, it wasn't now. Bryan Plat owned one in the next town which was still a part of Colby County. Bryan was another experienced veterinarian in Andrew's opinion. Not as many years of experience as Doc Cambria, though, with ten under his belt, he would certainly be able to handle anything that came his way. Andrew had seen him in action himself, having started his career fresh out of college as a veterinary technician in Bryan's practice.

Andrew considered the new circumstances now that Doc Cambria was potentially out of commission as the veterinarian contracted by the town. With the contract coming up for bid again in September, he hoped Bryan Plat would rebid this year and win this time around. He probably had more practical experience than this new Doctor Woodbridge.

His thoughts were cut short as one of the veterinary technicians brought the Yorkshire Terrier to him in the same carrier Andrew had delivered the dog in just yesterday afternoon. She set the carrier down on the examination table in the center of the room and gave Andrew a smile.

"Here's Mr. Zeus. Doctor Woodbridge will be in shortly."

Andrew opened the carrier door and extracted the little dog. He came willingly, tail wagging happily, tongue licking whatever part of Andrew's face he could reach. Placing him on the stainless-steel examination table, Andrew visually surveyed the dog. His nose picked up the odor of peaches. The Yorkie had been given a bath ridding him of the foul doggy smell prevalent yesterday. He looked better too, without all the dirty, shaggy, wiry coat sticking up every which way. The terrier nudged his hand. "Looking for a pat, bud?" Andrew started patting the dog's head, then switched to rubbing his ears. Zeus angled his head to catch Andrew's scratching just behind his right ear. "Like that, pal?" He continued to scratch the dog as he contemplated the recent developments.

As ACO he'd never worked with any other vet and wasn't relishing the change. Doc Cambria had been the town-appointed vet since the animal control service had been established thirty-seven years ago. In fact, he'd been instrumental in its development. Until Doctor Hannah Woodbridge came along, he had been the only veterinarian in the town of Colby, and the most experienced of three in the county.

Andrew thought fondly of a few shared experiences they'd had while serving the town's wayward animal population together. He chuckled to himself remembering the time they fished an opossum out of Mrs. Cartwright's garden cistern. Damn thing had grabbed on to the net, scrambled up the pole, right up Andrew's arm, over his shoulder and down his back before jumping to the ground and hightailing it out of the vicinity. Doc Cambria had laughed so hard Andrew was afraid he'd fall over and break a hip.

Abruptly, Zeus sat on his haunches, still reveling in the scratching of his ears. Andrew set to stroking his hand down the sides of the dog's body, earning himself a wet lick on his wrist.

Andrew's expression sobered. "You missed meeting a great vet, pal. Doc Cambria was one of the best. Now, he's gone." Gone. Which means the position for town veterinarian will actually be up for grabs for real this year. In just four months. He'd have to give Bryan a call and appraise him of the situation.

A curt knock on the door preceded its opening, and Doctor Hannah Woodbridge walked in, looking far different than she had yesterday. In fact, she didn't look anything like she did yesterday.

Andrew felt his scowl turn into something more like an open-mouthed gape. He couldn't take his eyes off her, even without the wet tee-shirt.

Hannah Woodbridge paused just inside the doorway, her long silky hair held back with a barrette, except for a few strands framing her lightly freckled face. The white of her lab coat accentuated her beautiful hazel eyes and long dark brown eyelashes. A stethoscope looped around her neck; she carried a mini-laptop computer.

"Hello Officer Kelly," she said as she placed the laptop on the counter, set the stethoscope beside it, and turned to stand on the opposite side of the examination table. Immediately, Zeus scurried over to see her, pawing at her clean, white lab coat, Andrew completely forgotten.

He grimaced before brightening into a reluctant smile. How could he not? Her own smile stretched ear to ear as she greeted the Yorkie. "Mornin' Doctor Woodbridge. I see Zeus is doing well."

Hannah continued to pat the dog, rubbing him from head to tail, causing him to shimmy with delight. "Yes, he's doing very well. His blood work is fine. He's well rested and he even smells better after his complimentary bath. He's ready to go."

Andrew looked her squarely in the eyes. "Good to hear." He gathered Zeus to him. Grabbing the carrier, he held open the door with one hand while balancing the dog with the other hand. A spark raced into his brain. *Should I mention the Malin case?* His hands paused at the thought.

Mistaking his hesitation, Hannah reached out. "Let me help you." She took the dog from Andrew and held him aloft while he got the carrier ready. Once the towels had been spread, Hannah placed the dog at the door to the carrier. Zeus walked inside, turned around and then walked to the closed door to look out at them, his ears drooping, his eyes sad.

"Hold on, Zeus. It's a short trip to the shelter. I expect your mama is already waiting for you there."

BID TO LOVE

Andrew glanced up and caught Hannah smiling at the dog in the carrier. He turned toward her smiling as best he could. "Ah, I wanted to congratulate you on your new position as Doctor Cambria's new associate. I finally got to see the memo." Slipping his hands in his pockets, he added, "It was quite a surprise to learn of Doctor Cambria's stroke yesterday. And your new position, of course."

Hannah picked up her laptop and hugged it to her chest. "Thank you. I'd like for us to establish a good working relationship."

"Me too. We should have a meeting to discuss some of the relevant issues." He picked up the dog's carrier.

Hannah frowned. "Such as?"

Andrew set the pet carrier back on the examination table. He thought of all the help Doc Cambria had given him to prosecute Myron Malin for animal abuse and neglect. "There's one major issue I have been following."

Hannah looked up, meeting his eyes with an intensity that made him speechless for a few seconds. "Ah, there's a man in town who has previously been charged with animal abuse and neglect. Although his previous dogs were removed from his custody, he's managed to obtain a new one. I have been keeping a close eye on the new dog."

Hannah's eyes widened. "Any signs of repeat behavior?"

He shook his head, "None so far. I don't hold out much hope. Leopards and spots and all that. I may end up needing you to evaluate the dog if it happens again."

"That's what I'm here for. Do give the man the benefit of a doubt. He might have seen the error of his ways."

Andrew shook his head vehemently. "Not this guy. It's only a matter of time."

Hannah stared at him a few seconds before clearing her throat. "Let's hope it doesn't come to that."

"Yes. In the meantime, thanks for taking care of Zeus. Stop by my office soon." Andrew gave her his best megawatt smile. "I'll give you the ten-cent tour."

Hannah blushed. "Only ten cents?" She reached behind her for her stethoscope and missed. Rolling her eyes and abandoning the awkward maneuver, she turned to give him her full attention.

"There's not much to show. I keep adding on as the town budget allows." He beamed again, shifting the carrier from one hand to another. *She's blushing. Hopefully with pleasure at my flirting rather than embarrassment.*

"I'll do that." Hannah bent down to look inside the carrier. "Have a safe trip, Zeus. And stay out of hot cars."

"Right." Andrew picked up the carrier. He extended his free hand to the attractive veterinarian. He was surprised to find her grip gentle but firm. In his experience most women had flimsy handshakes. He also was intrigued by the softness of her skin. *Is it this soft all over?* He hurried out the door, holding the carrier over his pelvis area so she couldn't see the change in the front of his pants. *I'm not falling for her. It can't happen.*

Hannah studied Officer Kelly's backside as he left the examination room before shutting the door behind him. She slumped against it, slowly letting out a long breath of air between her lips. He was far too handsome. But it was his eyes that stopped her breath. Big, brown, and soulful, like Blackie's. Thankfully, he seemed not to notice the affect he had on her. *Just as well. A mutual attraction would complicate everything. I have enough on my plate. Been there, done that and got the scars to prove it.*

Besides, she really needed to concentrate on learning to run the clinic, crash-course style. And she needed to learn their procedures and where everything was stored so she didn't have to keep asking everyone for things all the time. Most of all she needed to make this work. Buying this practice from Dr. Cambria was going to cost her a fortune.

On top of the two hundred thousand dollars in student loans she still owed for her undergraduate education and vet school. Soon, she would have the business loan for the practice to take on. She was a long way off from her dream of owning her own clinic. In the future, one day, she would write the final payment check and it would all be hers.

Shaking her head, Hannah rocked backward, grabbing her stethoscope, and stuffing it into her coat pocket before opening the door. "Where do I go next?" she asked of no one in particular.

CHAPTER THREE

Roslin Bank closed at five. Hannah was the last customer in the door. Her five o'clock appointment with Dean Merryweather, loan supervisor was supposed to be brief, so she could get back to the office for a last-minute six o'clock appointment. True to his word, Mr. Merryweather was waiting for her with the papers needing to be completed.

"Good afternoon, Doctor Woodbridge. Ready?" he asked.

"Ready as I'll ever be," Hannah said, pulling a pen out of her purse.

"Any last questions?"

Hannah reached for the first piece of paper Dean Merryweather was handing her. "No, I understand the terms and conditions."

They worked through each page together. Until he pulled her credit report.

He stared at it, sitting back in his chair, his expression suddenly closed.

Afraid to ask, but knowing she had to, Hannah set down her pen and sat on the edge of her chair. "Is there a problem?"

He turned the report around so she could read it. "You have a lot of personal loans already. Your debt-to-income ratio is exceedingly high."

A quivering started in Hannah's stomach. She sat forward perusing the numbers. "The personal loans are student loans. For college and vet school. I just started at the clinic. Doesn't that count?"

"Yes, of course. Your salary would allow you to live very modestly and pay for the business loan, but these student loans are going to require repayment soon. Based on these numbers, there's no way you can handle all that debt on the clinic's salary."

Hannah sat up straighter. "I understand. You are forgetting the appointment as town veterinarian. Doctor Cambria said that pays a lump sum. It comes up for re-appointment this September. I intend to use that money for the student loans."

Dean Merryweather steepled his fingers before his chest and looked at her. His eyes narrowed. "It's a competitive bid, is it not?"

The bottom dropped out of Hannah's stomach. "Yes, of course. But there's no reason why I shouldn't be selected."

"I'm sorry, Doctor Woodbridge. The bank can't give you the business loan until we are sure you receive the appointment."

"Even though it's only for a one-year term?"

" Typically, the town re-appoints the same person year to year as long as the bid is acceptable. So if you can win the bid, it's likely you'll hang on to it for as long as you want it." He leaned forward in his chair. "Win that bid and I will give you the loan."

"And if I don't?" she whispered.

Frowning, he sat back again. "Then I'm sorry."

Slumping back in her chair, Hannah stared at him for a few seconds before lowering her watery gaze to her hands in her lap. Then struggling to her feet, unsure if her wobbling legs would carry her, she thanked him for his time and left.

Silence met Hannah at the door to her apartment, as it did every evening. It was after eight. There had been no time for supper and despite her empty stomach, all she could think about was a hot bath and her soft bed.

The day had started out well enough, but the visit from Officer Kelly had been the only bright spot. By noon she'd fallen behind schedule. To catch up, she had worked through the half hour reserved for her lunch. An emergency in the early afternoon set her back again. A hit and run victim, a beautiful Pomeranian, had escaped with a fractured leg. Simple though it was, it took an hour to stabilize, set, and cast. Behind schedule again, she had lumbered through the rest of the afternoon, trying to soothe the feelings of peeved clients while concentrating on the health issues of her patients.

The gurgling of her gut intensified at the thought of a few of the harsh statements made about her lateness. Everything from "Doctor

Cambria was always on schedule" to "my time is just as valuable as yours, Doctor Woodbridge." Hannah felt her cheeks burn as she recalled the last statement. Even the explanation of an emergency did little to placate some clients, even though Hannah knew these same clients would expect her to prioritize their pet in the event of emergency regardless of how full the day's schedule. Then, the disaster at the bank, followed by rushing back to the clinic for a six o'clock appointment that was a no-show.

Do I really want to sign up for this? Maybe I'm being told something by the Big Guy. Maybe my being declined is a good thing. Maybe I'm not ready to take on this practice, financially, emotionally, or intellectually. I sure wish I had those five years with Doc Cambria to learn the ropes.

Hannah walked over to the small pile of mail she had placed on the kitchen counter when she first came home. Leafing through it for anything interesting, her eye fell upon the return address of a banking agency – the one that handled her student loans. She groaned, pulling that envelope out of the pile and tore it open. A crisp, white, single page slid out unevenly between her trembling fingers. With a heavy sigh, she unfolded the page.

Dear Ms. Woodbridge,

It has come to our attention that you are now gainfully employed. As a result, and in accordance with the regulations of the Student Loan Administration, it is now incumbent upon you to begin remittance of payments on your student loans.

Beginning on the first of September and each first of the month thereafter, you will be expected to remit a payment of $1250.34 toward repayment of said loans.

If your circumstances should change, please contact us immediately to re-evaluate the
loan repayment schedule.
Most sincerely,
Deborah Mitchell
Administrator, Student Loan Services

Hannah let the letter flutter back on the countertop and dropped her head into her hands. Twelve hundred dollars per month. It was far more money than she had anticipated. That was going to eat half of her take-home pay and leave her next to nothing to pay the business loan she'd have to take out. No wonder Dean Merryweather had balked at giving her the loan.

Scrubbing her face with her hand, she walked over to the living room window. Birds flew by, landing on her neighbor's birdfeeders. Hannah watched the birds fly in and out, taking what they could carry. An icy feeling doused her as she realized if she couldn't get the loan, Doc would have to sell the clinic to someone else and she'd have to leave Colby.

Frantically, she thought back to her interview with Doctor Cambria and the valuable advice he'd given her. It had all seemed possible back then. The clinic would pay her a reasonable salary which would cover her living expenses and allow her to make payments on the business loan she was going to need when she took over the clinic completely. The student loans would be covered by the town job. The contract could provide her with a twenty-thousand-dollar payment for services. It did not include materials and medications she would provide the animals as needed; those would be billed to the shelter. The twenty thousand dollars would be her fee for services rendered. She had hoped it would cover the student loans and allow for a new car. Now, it seemed like it would be just enough to meet the student loan bills with a tiny bit extra.

And the contract was coming up for renewal in four months.

She was going to have to make sure she won that contract.

"Well, I'll have to make it happen," she said as she walked back into the kitchen and reached for the wine bottle.

With a glass of wine in hand, she stepped outside behind the building. Between the light glare from the building and the crescent-shaped moon, it was hard to view the stars. Searching upward, she finally found Vega, a bluish-white star, part of the constellation

DIANA ROCK

Lyra. A streak of light, a falling star, caught her eye. Fingers crossed; she made a wish that she'd win the bid and her dream.

CHAPTER FOUR

Andrew pulled the white panel van out of its parking space at the shelter. This was his fifth year as animal control officer, and he was well acquainted with the procedures, responsibilities, and requirements. He loved working with the animals. Seeing them returned to their families, receiving the health care they desperately needed, and finding them forever homes were the highlights of his job.

Just as satisfying but harder was building a case against an owner for abuse or neglect, taking him or her to court and winning. Most of the time, because of his diligence, he won the case. Sometimes he was able to get the owner to surrender the animal before the case went to court. These cases were easier for him and the court system, but they had one disadvantage: the owner who surrendered before a hearing was never charged with animal abuse and neglect and entered into the state's database. It was the court's way of keeping track of repeat offenders. The list was also accessible by animal shelters, rescue groups, and any commercial entity selling animals. This helped to keep animals out of the hands of convicted offenders. Sometimes the offenders were not prohibited from having more animals, but any shelter or rescue group smart enough to know about the list wouldn't be allowing them access to another creature.

Andrew knew Myron Malin's name was on the list and yet, somehow, he had been able to acquire another dog.

He took a right out of the shelter's driveway, heading down the familiar road. A road he had taken every day now for the past five months. Down past Everett Lane, along Main Street to the other side of town. Over to the sparsely populated outskirts of town on the west end.

There, as every day, he slowed down while approaching the rundown and rusted trailer home of Mr. Myron Malin. The debris surrounding the trailer didn't change much day to day, though bags of trash appeared and disappeared beside the trailer door. It wasn't the condition of the yard or the trailer that brought Officer Kelly out to this end of town. It was the welfare of the occupant on the end of the metal chain attached to the rear bumper of the trailer that he came to see each day. A dog named Toby.

Andrew pulled the vehicle up to the side of the road in front of the trailer plot and picked up his binoculars from their place beside his seat, his breath tight in his chest. Staring down through the lenses, he spotted the light yellow dog, hiding himself in the shade of the trailer. Beside him were two plastic bowls. One looked like it might contain dog kibble while the other might hold water, or so it seemed from this distance. It was hard to tell from his angle of viewing and with the shadows under the trailer. He let out a fast breath.

As happy as Andrew was to see Malin was not being neglectful; leaving the dog in shade with food and water, he was equally pissed. The town's attorney had advised him to find a sign of abuse or neglect, rather than just contest Malin's ownership. If either or both were seen, just one more time, he would have a stronger cause to file with the court for seizure. One sign of neglect would do it. Just one. And he came every day looking for that one opening he needed to save that poor dog the misery of being on a six-foot chain, perpetually tied to that trailer bumper in all weather.

He set the binoculars down on the towel beside his seat. So much for today. He'd try again tomorrow. Signaling, he pulled out into the roadway, made a U-turn, and headed back into town. His next assignments were waiting for him: a missing cat report, bats in a chimney complaint, wandering dog on School Street near the high school and a bird inside the Catholic church. While he wasn't required to handle wildlife cases, Andrew always tried to make the initial contact and then recommended other services as needed.

Today, as often happened, his mind remained on the issue of Toby and the many dogs in similar circumstances. Andrew knew there was little he personally could do to save them all. Without cause, he couldn't fight for custody of every animal whose owner treated it in a manner Andrew didn't agree with. However, he could when probable cause gave him the right and responsibility to take the owner to court. Blood boiling and gut churning, Andrew smacked the steering wheel as the van sat in the driveway of Miss Rose's house.

Miss Abigail Rose, an elderly woman, came out of her house, scurrying to his open window. "Oh, thank God, you're finally here! I'm worried sick about Primrose!"

Andrew put his thoughts away and smiled at Miss Rose. "Don't worry, we'll look hard." A spot of orange caught his eye as he got out of the van. His eyes narrowed. A bright orange cat sat on the peak of the roof. "She wouldn't happen to be an orange tabby, would she?"

"Yes! Have you seen her?" Miss Rose clapped her hands together.

Pointing to the roof with one hand, he pulled his portable radio out of his holster with his other hand. "She's right up there. Do you have a ladder, Miss Rose?"

"Golly, no." Miss Rose pressed one hand to her heart while her other dabbed at her tearing eyes.

"Let me see if my friend, Dawson, at the fire department is willing to get her down for you."

Half an hour later, with the help of Colby's bravest, Primrose was securely in the arms of Miss Rose. As he packed up to leave, he spotted a Mini Lop rabbit hopping free on the neighbor's lawn. He turned to Miss Rose. "Miss Rose, is that your neighbor's rabbit?"

"Well, yes. And no. What I mean is, it was. They got it as a baby for the kids for Easter, but it got big, and the kids lost interest. They turned it loose. The poor thing has been hopping around the area all day." She snuggled her cat. "Maybe you should catch it and bring it to the shelter."

His teeth clenched and his blood seething, Andrew reached for the fetch pole. "I will catch it. But I can't keep it. There isn't space for rabbits. Or reptiles. Or rodents."

Abigail glanced up, a quizzical expression on her face. "You don't have room?"

Shaking his head, "No. I have plans to add on to the shelter, but not enough money to do it. And the town won't fund it."

"That's terrible." Clearly horrified, Miss Rose placed her hand over her heart. "What if someone donated the funds?"

"That would be great," Andrew said, his eyes glued to the rabbit. "When and if it happens. Excuse me, Miss Rose, while I go catch that bunny."

In minutes he had the ball of fluff in the back of his van.

Back on the road, this time en route to the bats-in-the-chimney call, Andrew resumed his musings. He needed to call Bryan. Pulling into the driveway at Gross Point Road, he pulled out his cell phone.

Dialing up the familiar number always sent a wave of nostalgia rolling through Andrew's heart. It had only been five years since he'd left though it felt much longer.

"Good Afternoon, Plat Veterinary Service. How can we help you today?"

It was the same voice that had been answering the phone during his tenure there.

"Mrs. Hopkins, how are you? It's Andrew Kelly."

"I know who this is! You are like a bad penny, young man. Didn't you just call last week?" the elderly woman cackled, bringing a smile to his face. Teresa Hopkins, the octogenarian receptionist, had a laugh that made everyone want to join in the merriment.

Andrew's heart lightened with her unfailing good mood. "I did. I wanted to let you all know about Doc Cambria."

BID TO LOVE

"How is the poor man? Have you seen him?" Her voice was threaded with concern. Doc Cambria and she went back a long time. It no doubt hit her hard to learn of his stroke.

"Not yet. I hope to soon." Her questions zinged him like an arrow in the chest. *Why hadn't I thought to visit? Or sent a card? Or something? What kind of friend and colleague am I to have neglected him?*

"Well, you give him my regards and tell him I've been praying for a complete recovery. He is such a nice man, and a great vet," she clucked.

Tucking the phone between his shoulder and ear, he pulling out his notepad and wrote "doc" on it in big, bold, letters. "I'm sure he'll be pleased to hear that."

Teresa's voice hardened as she got back to business. "What can we do for you today? No more bad news, I hope."

"No. I just need to talk with Bryan a moment if he can take my call. I'm going to try to get him out of the house tonight."

Teresa cackled again. "Oh, you troublemaker. What's your sister going to say about that?"

"I'm sure she'll have plenty to say about it. But I'm going to ask him anyway." Andrew chuckled. Mrs. Hopkins knew Kimberly well enough to know she wasn't going to like having her husband out after work instead of home with her and Daniel.

"Let me check with Dr. Plat, sweet cheeks. I'll see if he's free," and the line clicked to hold music. Andrew drummed his fingers on the steering wheel along with the percussion. When he was about to hang up, Bryan came on the line, his voice tired. "Yo, what's up?"

"Can you meet me for a beer at The Irish Harp tonight about seven? It's important but it won't take long."

A silent pause – "Yeah, I'll have to check in with the boss. I haven't been out in a while so it should be okay," he said, a note of trepidation in his voice.

Andrew felt for the guy. But Bryan had married his sister knowing her headstrong nature. He had warned him. "If I know Kimberly, she's going to be pissy about it."

Bryan groaned. "Well, pal, when is she not pissy about something. See you later."

Andrew disconnected the call and sat musing over the marriage between Bryan and Kimberly. It wasn't good. The whole situation, plus the memory of his parents' nasty and verbally abusive divorce had him believing to his core that marriage was something he wasn't interested in even trying. It was full of hardship and hate, conflict and, ultimately, ended with kids being hurt and forgotten.

The bar table wobbled when Andrew set his bottle of Pepsi down. *No wonder the table was unoccupied.* Glancing up, he saw Bryan approaching. Andrew stood to shake his hand.

"Hey bud. Give me a sec to get a beer," Bryan said, pumping Andrew's hand before letting go and disappearing toward the bar.

"Yeah, sure. No problem," Andrew said to his back. He sat down and let the fingers of his right-hand twirl the plastic bottle on the table. He concentrated on not making the table wobble as he did it and was successful until Bryan sat down.

The two men scanned each other across the Formica table top. Bryan took a swig of his Corona and wiped his mouth on his shirt sleeve.

"Nice," Andrew smirked.

"Shut up. You're not my mother or my wife." Bryan set the bottle down, shaking both bottles as the table shifted again.

Andrew rubbed his chin. "Bad day?"

"Bad week. And the wife's all bent I'm having this beer with you."

"Sorry. We could have met over coffee."

"Nah, I needed a beer. It's been too long. Besides, it has nothing to do with coffee or beer and everything to do with paying attention to her now that she's pregnant again." Bryan sat back in his chair, his grip on the beer tight. "So, what did you want to talk to me about?"

Andrew pressed forward, elbows on the table. "I wanted to talk to you about the bid."

"That? What about it? It's not for another three —four months, isn't it?"

Andrew glanced left, then right for any eavesdroppers before answering. "I wanted to know if you were interested in bidding this time with Doctor Cambria out."

"Yeah, heard about his stroke. I am planning to," Bryan replied. "What about it?"

"There's a complication." Andrew lowered his voice.

Bryan leaned in to hear better. "How so?"

"There's a chance Doctor Cambria's replacement is going to put in a bid."

"Who is that?" Bryan crossed his arms on the tabletop, leaning in further.

"Hannah Woodbridge."

Bryan took a swig of his beer and set it down again. He swallowed slowly, his eyes unfocused as he thought. "I don't think I know her."

"I'm not surprised. She's new to the area."

"What do you know about her?"

"Fresh out of school essentially."

"Doesn't sound like she'll be a problem. She doesn't have much practice experience."

"No. I don't think so either. Even so, I thought I'd give you a heads up." Andrew drained the last of his soda. "Still – she is an opponent."

"Great." Bryan said flatly. "I expect Paul Tabs will bid too."

"Is it that important to you?" Andrew asked, peeling the label off his damp bottle.

Bryan raised an eyebrow. "You mean, do I need the money?"
Andrew blinked and nodded.

"Yes. Kimberly wants a cruise to the Mediterranean next year. Lord knows I don't need any more business." Bryan also fiddled with the label on his bottle.

"Well – I hope you get it. After everything you did for me, you deserve it. Plus, you've waited a long time for this chance."

"Me too. I'd love to get your sister off my back about this cruise."

Andrew smiled. He was well aware of Kimberly's general attitude and how she responded when she got her head wrapped around an idea. Best to agree and get out of her way. Growing up, Kimberly, being the eldest sibling, had bossed him and his older brother Dale around mercilessly. Unchecked by divorced parents, it had become her most salient trait as an adult.

"Speaking of off my back, want to go for a ride with Dawson and me next Wednesday afternoon? I'm only in the office in the morning that day."

"How come? Something special going on?"

"Nothing special, I just need a break. I've been working six days a week, sometimes seven for almost three months now. Dawson's off shift that day too so it works." Bryan downed the last of his beer. "By the way, Kim doesn't know, so don't say anything about it, okay?"

"Yeah, sure. Want to try that Nitmuck trail in Chesterville?"

"Perfect. I've been itching to try out my new Ibis."

"A new trail bike? Awesome. Keep our fingers crossed there aren't any calls or emergencies for either of us."

Starting to reply, Bryan paused open-mouthed when Andrew's radio squawked.

Andrew listened intently for a few seconds, radio to his ear, then set it back in the holster on his right hip. "Sorry, got to go. Duty calls and all that."

BID TO LOVE

Bryan grabbed his forearm to stop him. "Let me know if you hear anything for sure about Woodbridge bidding on the contract."

"You bet. And good luck with the bid," he said, before heading for the exit. "I'll be rooting for you."

CHAPTER FIVE

"Knock, knock," Hannah called through the storm door of the Animal Control Office as she rapped on the door frame. No reply came from inside.

A brown dog with the face of a pit bull and the furry body of a poodle sauntered over to the door to greet her, doing little more than panting a hello. Hannah tried peering inside the tiny office. Nothing was visible but an oversized desk, littered with papers and stacks of books. On the opposite wall, a screen door was open, through which an endless stream of barking could be heard. *He's probably out in the kennel area checking on something.*

She eased the door open, being careful to not let the dog slip out and entered Officer Andrew Kelly's office. The dog followed quietly behind her, nose in the air, sniffing as Hannah walked. Coming to a stop in the center of the office area, Hannah bent down, offering her palm for inspection. The brown mutt sniffed once then licked it. Reaching out gingerly, Hannah pet the dog's chiseled head and was greeted with a wide grinning pant.

Hannah's eyes darted around the office. A bookshelf full of books on every subject from canine behavior to farm animal feeding requirements filled one wall. A smile crossed her face as she spun around looking at the snapshot pictures on the wall of dogs and cats. Pictures of animals that Officer Kelly had managed to reunite with their owner? The more sobering items sat on a shelf on the wall across from his desk; cremation urns, each with a framed picture. Hannah walked over to examine the pictures. A huge lump formed in her throat as she looked at the seventeen snapshots of cats and dogs. Animals whose time came to an end in the kennel? Hannah's heart squeezed tight with the thought.

"They were never claimed. I'm hoping someday I can find their rightful owner and pass on their remains." Andrew said in a low voice behind her.

Hannah nodded, wiping the mist from her eyes. She cleared her throat as she turned, "That is a wonderful idea. It's nice the town is willing to pay for the private cremations."

A faint blush shaded his cheeks. "The town didn't. I did." Andrew gestured toward the dog still licking her hand. "I see you've met Maggie Mae."

"It's a pleasure to meet you, Maggie," Hannah said before standing up straight.

The dog sat, sticking out a paw for a handshake.

Laughing, Hannah took it and gave it a little shake before patting the dog with the big brown eyes again.

There were a few seconds of quiet as Hannah turned around and she and Andrew stared at each other.

At last, Andrew motioned to a chair on the opposite side of his desk and they both sat down. "To what do I owe the honor of your visit?" he asked, sitting back in his chair, allowing it to rock under his lean frame.

"I was on my way back from a barn call, thought I'd stop in and see the kennels." Hannah said. "Get the lay of the land so to speak."

Andrew nodded slowly before throwing open his arms and saying "Here's my office. On the other side of that door there," he said pointing to a closed door on the far-left side of the office, "is the feline room. I keep the door closed to keep the barking noise down. Settles down the cats. It's the best I can do under the cramped circumstances."

"Mind if I take a look?" she asked, heading for the door without waiting for an answer.

"No, not at all." Andrew said, getting up from his chair to go with her. "While you're here there is a new cat and a rabbit that may need some attention."

"A rabbit? I didn't know you took rabbits too."

Andrew shrugged. "It's temporary. I'm holding her until a rescue group can pick her up. The cats are unnerved with her in the room and she's frightened being there."

"Okay, sure. I'll have a look. Let me get my bag." Hannah detoured out to her car and returned with her black doctor's bag. She found Maggie sitting outside the door of the feline room and Andrew inside with a cat in his arms.

After Andrew placed the cat on the small exam table, Hannah began her physical examination. Being very docile, the cat was cooperative. "I call her Freckles."

"Heart and lungs sound good, teeth are fair, maybe a cavity. Eyes are clear but the ears are inflamed. I see brown waxy secretions and smell an odor. Has she been scratching at the ears or doing a lot of head shaking?"

"Not that I have seen. Then again, I'm usually in the office area or the kennel."

"I see a few scratches on the backs of her ears, so she might have been scratching at them. Most likely ear mites. I'll have the clinic put up a bottle of ear meds you can pick up later today."

"Will do. Nothing else?"

"No, that's it," Hannah said, stroking the cat from head to tail.

Andrew took the cat from the table and placed it back in its compartment. A Mini Lop came out next. The rabbit stuck its head into the crook of Andrew's elbow, hiding its face, playing the if-I-can't-see-you-then-you-can't-see-me game. He held on to the fluff ball as Hannah did a quick exam.

"She looks to be fine. Anything in particular you want me to check for?" She glanced up, her fingers stroking the rabbit's softness, her fingertips grazing Andrew's arm.

He stared into her eyes, her face just inches away. Hannah felt his eyes on her lips. His head shifted as though he would kiss her. The Lop squirmed in his arm, trying to break free. They both reached for it, bringing them even closer together. Once the bunny held still, Hannah puffed out a sigh and stepped back.

"That was close," she said. "Anyone else you want me to look at while I'm here?" She began putting her instruments back in her bag.

"No." Andrew quickly released the rabbit back into its cage.

Hannah grasped his forearm and stopped him. A tingle zipped through her body at the feel of his skin. Their eyes met in the silence of the moment before Hannah released him. "Um, why can't you keep it?"

Andrew gestured around the small room. "There's no place here for a rabbit. I close this shower curtain to keep the rabbit from the prying eyes of the cats." He pulled a blue solid vinyl curtain around the rabbit's cage. "I certainly can't put it in the kennel area. Maybe someday I'll be able to build an addition for critters like rabbits and rodents and reptiles. I put construction money in my budget request every year, but it never makes it to the town budget. The Police Commission vetoes it. So, for now, I have no place to hold them for longer than a few hours." Andrew walked out of the room.

Nodding, Hannah grabbed her bag. After a brief glance around, she returned to the office where Maggie patiently waited. Andrew motioned toward the kennel door with his left arm, and they all headed out to the dog kennel area.

A cacophony of barking erupted when the trio entered the kennel area. Ten six-by-eight kennels ran both sides of the aisle, only half of them occupied. Hannah was pleased to see the neat and clean condition of the kennels, both those in use and the empty ones.

The dogs seemed in good spirits, even though they were cooped up. Each kennel had a door that led to an outside area, where the dogs could get some fresh air.

"I guess you don't have air conditioning here," Hannah picked at the front of her button-down shirt and fanned it.

Andrew smiled and dropped his chin to his chest. "Well, truth to tell, I have air conditioning in the office, but the dogs' kennels don't. So I don't like to run it. I turn it on in the feline room, not in the office," he said. He toed a scuff mark on the tile floor. "Doesn't seem fair."

Hannah smiled. "No, I guess it wouldn't."

Walking back into the office, Hannah headed for the screen door. "I really should get back to my own office and leave you to your work. Did you have any questions or concerns about any of your other guests?"

"No, no concerns. But I would like to discuss that issue with you in more detail."

"What issue is that?" Hannah's head tilted.

Andrew motioned for her to sit down again and resumed his seat behind the desk.

"I wanted to talk with you some more about Mr. Malin. About a year ago, we served a warrant on him for the seizure of his three dogs. Chief complaint was animal neglect and abuse. All three animals were malnourished, unvaccinated, left for days without food or water in the hot sun. It's a wonder they survived as long as they did." Andrew scrubbed the scruff on his chin before continuing. "Court ordered seizure, all three dogs were seized, returned to health and adopted out to good homes. I'm happy to say they are all doing very well now."

"But..." Hannah cocked her head to one side.

"Now he has another dog. Yellow lab mix breed. Keeps it tied to his trailer home's bumper, so it crawls under the trailer for shade. Far as I can tell he has food and water bowls every day. Hard to tell from the distance what's in them, even with binoculars." Andrew got up and paced the small space a few times before continuing. "I'm just concerned the same thing will happen. Myron Malin is an alcoholic. Currently, he seems to be on the sobriety wagon but when he gets off, I'm afraid for the dog. I just want you to be aware of the situation so that when it finally hits the fan, we'll be on the same page when it comes time to go to court to seize the animal." He returned to his desk and sat down. Maggie sat down beside him.

Hannah rose. She placed her hands on his desk and leaned over invading his personal space. "First, I'm sorry to hear Mr. Malin has such a bad reputation. I'm glad his three dogs were seized and rehabilitated. Don't presume to include me automatically in any plans you have to seize this new dog of his. If there is just cause, I will be more than happy to assist you in petitioning the court. But do not consider my involvement to be a foregone conclusion." Hannah snapped straight up.

Andrew sat up straighter. "Doc Cambria was extremely helpful with Mr. Malin. He was happy to assist me in every way possible."

Hannah stared Andrew squarely in the eyes, her teeth clenched. "I'm not Doctor Cambria. I will help where I see fit and reasonable. But I will not stick my nose into other people's business unwarranted."

"It's your job as town-appointed veterinarian." Andrew reminded her.

"It's my job to see to the welfare of the animals here at the kennel and in the community and to assist in the writing of animal protection laws for the town of Colby. I will see to the welfare of Mr. Malin's dog, but I will not single him out for a witch hunt for his previous behavior." Hannah turned on her heels, heading for the screen door.

Andrew rushed from behind the desk, his hand reaching out and catching Hannah's forearm. "Wait – there's something else I wanted to talk to you about."

Hannah stopped, clutching her vet bag to her chest. Her eyes were wary. The emotions from the last argument still affecting her. "Well," she said. "I haven't all day."

He huffed out a sigh, clearly trying to rein in a response. "I wanted to ask you about the job as town-appointed veterinarian. The appointment runs out soon."

"Yes, I'm aware of that," Hannah said, clutching the bag a little tighter. "Bids are due in a month or so."

"Right. I was wondering if you'll be bidding or if Doc Cambria will be?"

Hannah's eyes narrowed. "Doctor Cambria is effectively gone from the practice. I'm buying him out. So, I'll be the one presenting a bid."

"Do you think that's smart? I just wonder if it might be too much with a new practice to run and all."

Hannah dropped her bag on the floor at her feet. "Let's get this straight right now. I will be bidding, and I will win that bid." Hands on her hips, she sidled up to him, stopping within a foot of Andrew's nose. "And I'll do a damn good job."

Andrew rested back against his desk, as if to give himself some personal space. "Okay, I get it."

"Don't you think I'm doing a good enough job now?" Hannah demanded, face red and fists clenched at her sides.

"Yes, yes of course it seems you're doing fine," Andrew said throwing up his hands, palms forward. "I'm just asking for a — a friend — who also wants to bid on the contract."

Stepping back as if she had been slapped, Hannah put space between them, nearly tripping backward over her vet bag. "Who? I didn't think there were any other vets in town," she said, stumbling to remain upright.

"There aren't in Colby. Bryan Plat is in Wilkesbury, next town over," Andrew said, resettling himself of the edge of the desk. "He was bidding against Doc for years. Doc always got the job, so Bryan quit bothering. Bryan feels he has a chance now. He's definitely going to bid on the contract."

Hannah picked up her vet bag and advanced on Andrew. "Just because he's been trying for the job doesn't give him the right to it now. You can tell Bryan it's my job to lose. And I don't intend to do any such thing." She turned, heading for the door. The audacity of both men to instantly assume she would give it up because Bryan had wanted it for years. The town-appointed vet job was too important to her financial plan to lose. She had no intention of letting anyone else take it.

CHAPTER SIX

Watching her walk to her older model Corolla, Andrew fumed. He wished the town could change veterinarians now. Bryan Plat was interested in the job, would even take it on early if needed. It would be great to work together again.

Picking up his cell phone, he dialed Bryan's personal phone number. There was no answer, so he left a message. "Hey bud, it's me, Andrew. Hannah Woodbridge is definitely bidding. Thought I'd let you know. Talk to you soon. Bye."

Andrew disconnected the call and turned back toward his desk. He had a few things to take care of before he left tonight. He sat down as Maggie Mae walked over beside him.

Andrew slumped back in his chair, dropping his hand to pet Maggie's head. Her soft curls slipped through his fingers like silk. Working with Doc had been so much easier. They had gotten along well, often thinking the same thing at the same time. Clearly, that type of relationship was not going to transpire between Hannah and himself. And he couldn't be more unnerved, especially considering his body's reaction to the attractive vet.

If only Andrew could talk the boss into speeding up the bidding process. Or perhaps doing an emergency reappointment. Maybe he could get Bryan into the job faster. There was only one thing to do.

Andrew picked up the telephone and dialed. "Hello, Susan. Any chance I can get in to see the chief?"

***

The apartment door hadn't even shut yet from the backward kick of her foot when Hannah's purse and lunch bag hit the floor. Reaching behind her, she unclasped her bra, releasing a loud woosh of relief as it gave way. Another audible sigh as her feet slipped out of her shoes and hit the squishy carpet. She glanced over at the window. The street lights were on, haloing in the humid summer heat.

Slumping down on the couch, her bones melted into the soft cushions as she stretched out.

The moment her head connected with the pillow her cell phone chimed. Grumbling, she hoisted herself upright and reached for it. A quick glance at the screen gave her a boost of energy. She clicked the button, connecting to the call. "Cortland, hi."

"Well, hello stranger. How's everything going? I haven't heard from you and you promised to keep me posted."

Hannah's head sank into her palm. "I know, I'm sorry. Things have kind of imploded and I'm trying to keep my head above water." Tempted to flop back on the couch, but afraid she'd fall asleep in the middle of the call, Hannah heaved herself up and paced to the window.

"What's going on? I thought you were setting up your apartment and breaking into the routine slowly with Doctor Cambria."

"Oh, Cort. Doctor Cambria had a stroke two days after I got here. So instead of selling me the clinic a couple years from now, he and his wife are selling it now. I've got the entire business all on my own."

"Jiminy, so you're handling the entire operation all by yourself?" Her voice expressed incredulity.

"Yeah. Seven days a week, ten to fourteen hours a day. I can't remember ever being this tired in my life." Walking to the fridge she pulled out a half empty bottle of wine and poured herself a generous glass. The cold Pinot Grigio would soothe more than her parched throat.

"Can't you get any help?"

"Not right now. I'm still trying to get the business loan, so I need the balance sheet and expenses to look good."

"Crap," Cortland muttered.

"On top of all that, my student loan repayment plan starts soon." Swigging back a gulp of wine, Hannah sat back down on the couch.

"There's some other variables but suffice to say if I don't get a contract renewed with the town, I can't get the business loan and I'm toast."

"Can't you put off the student loans?"

"No, I've already put them off for six months prior. If I don't start making payments on the day prescribed, they'll go after my parents' house. They co-signed my loans and it's the only asset they have. You know they can afford those payments even less than I can." A sick feeling flourished in her stomach. Was it the wine or the topic?

"There must be something good happening? A bright side?"

The eternal flame of hope, Cortland Stewart always sought out the bright side of any bad situation. Somehow, she always managed to find at least one, no matter how remote.

"The people are nice, well, nearly all the people, anyway."

"Hmm, let me guess, the thorn is a guy."

"How'd you guess? The town's animal control officer isn't thrilled I'm replacing Doctor Cambria."

Cortland paused before replying. "Is it a sexist thing?"

Hannah took another gulp of wine. "No, not that I see. He's got a vet buddy in the next town he'd rather see have the job. Though he might be wary of my lack of experience." She was silent a few seconds before adding, "Hey, enough about me. What's up with you?"

Clicking her tongue, a habit Hannah was familiar with from the years the two had lived together during vet school, Cortland spilled. "No change. It feels so strange to be back home under my parents' roof. I miss our apartment."

"I miss it too, even though what I have now is nice enough. Small but at least the neighbor slash landlady is a sweet little old lady. Any job prospects?"

"A few Skype interviews. The jobs are either in places I don't want to move to, or the pay is ludicrous. One guy offered me minimum wage and kept calling me 'honey.'"

"Yikes."

"I kid you not. And I can't wait to get out of here either. The atmosphere is worse, or it seems worse. Was it always this bad?"

"Your brother still there?"

"Oh yeah. Greg is still home, still unemployed, still playing Xbox live ten to fourteen hours a day. He's not leaving any time soon.

"Survivor's guilt?"

"No doubt about it. Jessica's death hit everyone hard, but he was closest to her. I think he's afraid to leave my mom alone. Like he feels responsible for her now that both Jess and I aren't home anymore." Cortland sighed. "It's not healthy."

Alarm bells rang in Hannah's brain, and she froze mid-step. "Are you okay? Did you relapse?"

"No, I'm okay. It's just a stressful environment on top of a stressful job-hunting situation. The sooner I'm out of here the better."

"It'll happen. You'll find a job soon. You were in the top ten of the class."

Cortland cleared her throat. "Hey, I'll let you go so you can get some R&R. You're probably exhausted from work."

"Yes. I just got home when you called." Hannah glanced at her watch. 9:38 PM. Nearly time for bed.

"Okay, I'll call you again soon."

"Yes, please do." Ending the call, Hannah plugged her phone into its charger, slugged back the last of the wine and went to bed.

CHAPTER SEVEN

Closing the door behind him as he entered, Andrew gave the police chief's office a quick glance. He'd only been here twice before; once for his interview for the ACO job and one time for a chewing out about a mishandled call. Or so the chief declared it. Andrew still felt the call had been handled correctly. It was just that he and Chief Dixon had a difference of opinion on what the correct handling of a situation should have been. The chief thought Andrew should have shot the dog dead before asking questions as to why it was frothing at the mouth. If he had, Mr. Anderson's dog would have been killed after licking a bad-tasting toad.

The office was the same as the last time he was there. Bookshelves filled the wall behind the desk, a behemoth of oak scattered with more papers and manila folders than Andrew's. The chief sat behind his desk, poking at his cell phone.

"Thanks for seeing me, chief." Andrew said.

The chief held up one index finger, then returned to poking at his phone.

What the heck is he doing? Trying to type an email or text message? Walking around the office, Andrew kept himself occupied reading the plaques and pictures on the wall.

Chief Dixon set the cell phone on his desk. "There. What can I do for you, Officer Kelly? If you're here about the addition to the shelter, I'm sorry. It didn't make the budget again."

Andrew's heart sank. He wasn't expecting that news. Shoulders slumped, he walked back to the desk and motioned toward the chair for permission to sit, Chief Dixon nodded. The rickety unpadded oak chair squeaked in protest under Andrew's lean form.

"I wanted to discuss a problem I'm having."

"What's going on, Kelly?"

Andrew shifted his weight in the chair causing it to creak again. "Sir, the new veterinarian. Doc Cambria's replacement. She's not working out as well as the old one."

"Explain. Is she not doing her job, not seeing the animals?"

"No, it's not that. She has been seeing the animals I bring in without a problem. She isn't as willing to help in incidents of neglect."

Chief Dixon sat up straight in his chair and pushed aside his cell phone. "You have incidents of neglect and she's not helping you?"

"Well, no sir. Not yet. But she has already made it clear she won't just rubber stamp any situation that I find. She wants to think about it and decide for herself. Sir, I know another veterinarian who's willing to cover —"

"Officer Kelly," Chief Dixon started to rock in his office chair. He snatched up a pen, stuck it between two of his fingers, and began tapping the top of his blotter as he thought. "I know you had a great working relationship with Doc Cambria for years. This new doctor, whatshername –"

"Doctor Woodbridge."

"This Doctor Woodbridge is his assistant or associate or whatever. Point is, she's covering for him in his business. The contract allows that. In so doing, she is covering the services for the Animal Control Office and the town." He pointed the pen straight at Andrew. "If he hadn't found coverage, we could appoint someone. But he did. So, unless you have a real complaint, an actual situation where she wasn't cooperative, I can't help you."

Andrew checked out his shoes, listening to his one chance hit the wall. Heat swelled under his armpits and around his collar. There wasn't much else for him to say. If the chief wouldn't support him, he was just going to have to suck it up. And hope that when the time came, like he anticipated it would with Myron Malin, Doctor Woodbridge would come through for him and the dog on the end of that six-foot chain.

Then he thought of one last person who might be able to help with the situation.

Glaring fluorescent lights blazed in the hallways of the Gentle Manor Nursing Home. The glossy linoleum floor formed an endless corridor from which thick-doored rooms branched off to the left and right. Andrew stopped in front of the door labeled 146. His hand reached out to knock on the half open door, then froze. Was this what he really wanted to do? Besides coming to see his old friend and co-worker, he knew it would be a little awkward to be asking questions about Doc's replacement. Perhaps if he concentrated on visiting Doctor Cambria, the topic would somehow come up on its own. Then he wouldn't have to feel like a slug for asking about her suitability for the job.

His knock sounded loud in the quiet corridor. Just as he was beginning to wonder if Doc was awake, a voice invited him in. Andrew pushed the door open, walking into the stale-smelling room. Ten steps in, he caught his first glimpse of the man who vaguely resembled Doctor Cambria. The old man's eyes brightened with recognition as Andrew approached the hospital bed.

"Andrew! It's so good to see you, my boy," the elderly man said as he held out his right-hand. "Thanks for the card and note!"

Grasping the hand and giving it a gentle shake, Andrew said, "Yes sir, it's great to see you looking so well."

With a stiffly-held left arm, Doctor Cambria motioned for Andrew to sit in a chair beside the bed.

"How are you feeling, doctor?" Andrew asked, taking a seat.

"Better, thank you for asking. I'm doing much better. Though the left arm and leg are still not cooperating fully yet. I'm working on it," he said, giving Andrew a lopsided smile.

"Good to hear, no, I mean, I'm glad you're getting better," Andrew stuttered.

The two men stared at each other for a few seconds.

"How's the shelter doing?"

Andrew shifted in his chair. "It's been fine. Fairly quiet."

"And Malin?" Doctor Cambria shifted his blankets, smoothing out the wrinkles.

"So far so good. Toby appears to be getting what he needs."

"Hmm. Keep an eye on that one." He waggled his right index finger. "He's bound to relapse."

"Yes, sir."

Doctor Cambria shifted again in his blankets. "So, how's my associate working out?"

Andrew rose and walked the few steps to the opposite wall and then turned back. "Well, sir, she seems to be a fine veterinarian. I'm just a little uncomfortable with her level of cooperation."

A slow, crooked smile spread across Doctor Cambria's face. "So, Doctor Woodbridge is showing her gumption, is she?"

Walking back to his seat Andrew shrugged. "I guess you could say that," he said hesitantly as he sat down on the edge of his seat, his eyes intent on the doctor. "She's certainly an independent thinker."

The doctor laughed easily. When he finished, he swiped his forehead with his right hand. "She's got spunk. That's what I like about her. And, of course, her qualifications."

"Which are, what exactly, if you don't mind my asking."

Doctor Cambria smiled again and nodded toward Andrew. "She was in the top five of her class at Cornell, did several internships, one in a rural animal practice and one at a mobile large animal practice.

"I am here to ask you to appoint someone else as your substitute as town vet. Until the new appointment in September. I don't know that she's especially suited for shelter practice."

"Are you kidding me? She studied shelter medicine in vet school and her last internship was with a large shelter outside of Chicago. She's got plenty of experience with shelter medicine."

Doctor Cambria's head tipped to the side, and he grinned lopsided at Andrew. "What's the real reason you're having difficulty accepting her?"

Andrew heaved a sigh. He stared down at his clasped hands in his lap, pausing to give himself a moment before answering. "I guess I'm just worried she can't handle the workload."

"Don't you worry about Hannah Woodbridge. She may have a soft heart but she's a smart veterinarian. She's doing well at the clinic from what I hear, and she'll do good by the shelter too. The contract is up in a few months. She can handle it."

"I hear she'll bid."

"It's part of her business plan to keep the town contract. I expect her to submit a bid when the time comes."

Andrew nodded in acknowledgement. So, his friend, Bryan Plat would have stiff competition when the bidding came up in September.

"Don't worry, my boy. Everything will all work out in the end," Doctor Cambria said before yawning. "Just give her a fair chance, Andy. That's all I ask."

Andrew knew he was beaten. He could only watch Doctor Woodbridge have her chance and let fate have its way. September wasn't too far away. Then it would be up to the town selection committee to decide who was the best candidate for the job.

CHAPTER EIGHT

The old Corolla pulled into the parking lot of the shelter at seven in the evening. A hard-packed dirt lot similar to the one at her own office, the car's tires kicked up clouds of dirt that lingered even as the car came to a halt before the drab brown building.

Hannah sat a couple minutes behind the wheel, trying to get her head together and calm the gallop of her heart. She closed her eyes and prayed for strength to the animal deities she hoped were out there. Prayed for the dog she had come to see and whose life she had been called to take away. It was, for any veterinarian, the worse possible service. If the animal were severely injured or desperately sick with no hope for recovery, it was hard enough. Incidents like today were even harder. Taking the life of a perfectly healthy and good animal purely because their time was up and no one had found it enough: pretty, handsome, playful, or friendly enough to take home and make their own beloved pet.

When she placed a bid on the services as town veterinarian, Hannah knew her job might, at some point, require this service. Here it was, not two weeks into covering the contract and she was already having to euthanize a perfectly healthy dog.

This had been part of her training at vet school. Her stint in the shelter medicine course been a heart-wrenching and eye-opening experience. Today's requirement was something she had experienced during her internship with a huge veterinary practice outside of Chicago. It had been her least favorite, as it was for one hundred percent of her classmates.

The taking of a life always aroused in her the memories of her childhood dog, Blackie who had been put down after suffering injuries in a hit and run accident. It was the start of Hannah's quest to become a veterinarian, her determination to cure and heal as many animals as she could. All in the name of Blackie. As much as she loved him, she understood now, his injuries were too severe to keep him alive at that time in veterinary medicine. Even if money had been available to treat him, he would have suffered significantly. It had been the humane thing to do though it wasn't so easy for a seven-year-old Hannah to understand at the time.

Today's event was not humane in Hannah's eyes. It was neat and tidy, but it did not feel humane. There was nothing she could do except fulfill her obligation to the town as required by the contract and silence her heart while doing so. There would be plenty of time to cry about the action after she left.

Hannah beat her hands on the steering wheel and lay her head on the backs of them. She prayed to Saint Francis of Assisi to comfort and care for the dog she was sending his way. Only then did she get out of her car with her black doctor's bag in hand.

At the door to the Animal Control Office, she knocked, after finding the door locked. *Of course, it's locked, it's after hours.*

The door swung open to reveal an equally downcast Officer Kelly. From the puffy redness around his eyes, Hannah could tell this evening's task was no easier for him than it was for her. After all, he had been caring for the dog for one hundred and eighty days. Feeding her, cleaning her kennel, letting her out, assuring her good health and welfare. It had to be even harder on him than it would be on herself. Hannah tried to redirect her focus toward seeing to Officer Kelly's emotional state rather than her own as a means of coping with the situation.

"Come in," was the only thing Andrew Kelly said as he backed away from the doorway. This time, Andrew led her, wordlessly, into a side room that held an examination table. Also, in the corner of the room was a large dog bed. Hannah felt her heart jolt at the sight. Never before had she seen so comfortable looking a final resting place for any dog. She made a huge mental note to do the same in her own practice starting tomorrow. All animals deserved to die in comfort instead of on the cold stainless-steel surface of an office examination table.

Andrew turned toward her and gestured toward the exam table. "You can set up your stuff here." His voice cracked as he added, "I'll go get her." Curtly, he turned and walked out of the room.

Setting her bag on the table, Hannah began pulling the two vials of drugs from her bag along with the two syringes. Next, she pulled out the intravenous port she would insert first into the dog's vein. It would be into this port that the two medications would be administered. First the sedative drug and then the lethal dose. Focusing on setting up as she had been taught to do, Hannah managed to stay dry-eyed and professional.

Until Andrew returned with the dog.

It was Maggie.

Maggie Mae, the poodle-pit bull cross, with the mass of chocolate brown colored poodle curls, stocky body and face of a pit bull, a poster dog of the mismatched crossbreed. She came through the door with Andrew like she was going out for a walk in the park, all happy and smiling. She walked over to Hannah, who had bent down without thinking, to greet her charge. Maggie Mae licked Hannah's hand first, then started licking her cheek which had suddenly become wet with tears.

"Not Maggie!" Hannah recoiled, her face a mirror of Andrew's, pinched with anguish.

Andrew nodded; his lips pressed tightly together.

Kneeling beside Maggie Mae, Hannah searched Andrew's eyes. She saw the same misery and frustration. No words were needed to describe their collective feelings.

Clearing her throat first, Hannah said, "Are you sure there's nothing else that can be done to keep her longer?"

Andrew's eyes flashed and hardened. "Of course, there isn't. Do you think I'd have called you over here if there wasn't any other choice?"

Hannah shook her head slowly, eyes downcast and focused on the dog's curly-topped massive head. "Okay," she said before taking a deep breath and letting it out.

Leading the dog over to the cushiony dog bed, Andrew got her to lie down. Hannah steeled herself. She reached for the first injection, giving Maggie Mae the mild sedative that would make her comfortable.

Turning away so Andrew would not see the tears in her eyes, Hannah readjusted the positions of the remaining materials on the examination table.

"I'm sorry I snapped at you." Andrew said from his position down on the floor at Maggie's side.

"No, I'm sorry. I never should have questioned your judgement. Of course, this is the last resort." Hannah rummaged in her bag for nothing in particular. She just had to remain busy. She couldn't look at Maggie Mae, or Andrew for that matter. Maggie's temperament reminded her of Blackie so strongly, she could barely stand it. Hannah could feel her heart tearing in her chest every time she looked at Maggie Mae and thought of the task she was here to perform.

Andrew cleared his throat. "S-she's feeling pretty mellow."

Hannah turned around to find Maggie Mae lying down in the comfortable dog bed, her head resting on Andrew's knee as he stroked her head with his left hand.

Steeling herself with a big breath, Hannah grabbed the intravenous plug and knelt down beside the dog. She deftly inserted it into the vein in the dog's left front leg. Maggie Mae licked her hand after the plug was in place, causing Hannah's heart to ache even more.

She turned her back on the dog and reached for the last syringe. Hannah turned back around and knelt down beside Maggie Mae and patted the dog's head. Maggie responded with more licks and tried to roll over onto her back for a belly rub. Hannah used her free hand to give the poor dog the best belly scratch she could under the circumstances. Then, as Andrew held her leg with the port as steady as his shaking hand could hold it, Hannah pulled the cap off the syringe just as Maggie Mae licked her arm again. Hannah quickly recapped the syringe, the drug not administered.

Andrew knelt straighter. "What are you doing? Why didn't you—"

"Because I just thought of a way to save her life," Hannah said, as she got up and put the syringe back on the examination table.

"H-how?" Andrew's voice cracked.

"I'll adopt her."

"W-what?" Andrew stuttered.

"I'll adopted Maggie Mae. I've wanted to get a dog once my practice was established. Why not Maggie?" Hannah glared.

Andrew stared back, eyes wide, mouth open but silent.

"Give me an adoption form," Hannah ordered.

Getting up off his knees, Andrew went into his office, where he rummaged on his desk before returning with the form.

By then, Hannah had removed the intravenous port from Maggie's leg and replaced it with a bandage.

Andrew handed Hannah the adoption application. Once filled out, Andrew took it and Hannah's check for fifty dollars. He stamped the form and said, "Congratulations, you now own Maggie Mae." Andrew held out his hand which Hannah took to shake. He held on, not letting her go. "I can't thank you enough for saving Maggie. I'm very grateful. She's very dear to me."

"She deserves a home and a life. A life as long as I can make it." Hannah let her hand rest in Andrew's grasp. Her hazel eyes stared into his dark brown eyes, reading the love he had for the dog at her feet. She gave his hand a little squeeze and he released her.

A huge smile broke out on Hannah's face as she took her bag in one hand and the end of Maggie's leash in the other hand. Andrew held open the door for the departing couple.

Maggie Mae wobbled as she strolled to Hannah's Corolla. Hannah lifted the woozy dog into the back seat, but Maggie instantly slid between the two front seats to sit in the front passenger seat. Hannah began to object, "Oh no, you belong in the back where it's safer."

The dog wouldn't budge. Nothing Hannah did could get the dog to return to the back seat: not pleading, pulling, or even the temptation of a treat.

At last, Hannah threw up her hands and got back into the driver's seat. "I guess I should be grateful you don't want to drive. But tomorrow, you get a seatbelt." Maggie glanced over at her, smiled, and started panting. "All right then, let's go home." Hannah started the car and drove away, leaving a visibly amused and relieved Andrew Kelly on the doorstep of the shelter.

***

"So, what's good here?" Cortland flashed a glance at Hannah over the top of her menu.

"Everything, so I hear. Though I can only vouch for the vegetarian and vegan items." She placed her menu beside her place setting.

Both women sat back in their chairs as the waiter delivered cocktails. Lifting her Fuzzy Navel to eye level, Cortland said, "Here's to your new job."

Hannah raised her Cosmopolitan, clinking her glass with Cortland's. "Thanks, BFF." She took a sip before adding. "And thanks for coming to visit. Sorry my couch isn't very comfortable."

"You sounded like you needed a cheer-up visit. And it's only for a couple nights. I can handle the couch for a couple nights." Cortland took a hearty sip. Her eyes widened as she swallowed hard, then her mouth opened as though blowing smoke rings. "Yikes! My chest and feet just sprouted hair! No wonder you ordered yours easy on the liquor."

"Yeah, they're pretty generous on the pour. There's no way I could handle an emergency after drinking one of these at full strength." Hannah set her martini glass down on the bar napkin. "So tell me. How's it going?"

"Really?" Cortland's face screwed up tight. She took another big gulp of her drink, avoiding Hannah's eyes. Setting the glass down on the tabletop but not letting go she fingered the stem. "It sucks. I mean. Everyone is nice enough to each other. Downright cordial. Daddy's as happy as he can be to have me home, but he's worried about how my mental health is being affected."

"And your mom?" Hannah's eyes never left Cortland's face.

"What can I say?" She paused as if searching for the right words. Then her eyes pierced Hannah's. "I'm not Jessica. And nothing anyone does for that matter will bring her back."

"Is she still going to church every day?"

Nodding, Cortland let go of the glass. "She goes to church every morning at seven o'clock, Monday through Friday, before she goes to work. Jessica died without getting last rights." Wiping a tear away before continuing, Cortland added, "Mom thinks Jess can't get into heaven because of it. Nothing the priest says can convince her otherwise."

Hannah sat back in her chair. The two women stared at each other across the table. Cortland's face crumpled, her brows drawn together, her eyes blinking madly. Reaching across to her friend, she placed her hand over Cortland's. "I'm sorry."

Cortland swiped away another stray tear. "It is what it is. I don't know who's worse: Mom or Greg." Sipping at her drink this time she set it carefully down. "The sooner I find a job and get the heck out of there the better. Even Daddy thinks so."

The waiter who took their order brought Hannah's Greek salad and Cortland's bacon cheeseburger, breaking the weight of the conversation.

"What about you? You mentioned tangling with the ACO. Still having problems with him?"

Hannah rolled her eyes but said nothing.

"What's that look mean?" Cortland wiped her fingers on her napkin. "What's his name again?"

"Andrew Kelly." Heat rose up Hannah's neck and face at the mention of his name on her lips.

"Are you blushing?" Cortland asked with a note of incredulity in her voice. "I've never seen you blush, girlfriend!"

Shooting her a death stare, Hannah kept eating.

A dawning smile spread across Cortland's face. Her voice dropped to a whisper. "Your face is on fire, Hannah. Did you sleep with him?"

"No!" She protested strongly enough people around them looked over. Whispering back, she added. "He's attractive and charming when he wants to be, and we have had a few moments."

"I hope it lasted more than a moment!" Cortland guffawed before chomping on another French fry.

"I'm happy to see you eating well. Have you had any binging and purging episodes since being home?"

"No." Cortland cocked her head and narrowed her eyes. "Nice try at redirecting. We were talking about you. What happened with Andrew Kelly?" She popped another French fry in her mouth.

Hannah rolled her eyes. "Oh, nothing happened. Not going to happen. I don't have time for that. Besides, he's still adamant about his friend getting the appointment as town vet." Hannah squared her shoulders before reaching for a dinner roll.

"Okay, so he's not on your side. He's hot. Enjoy the moments."

The heat drained from Hannah's face. "It's too dangerous." She picked the roll apart leaving a pile of crumbs on her bread plate.

Setting down her fork, Cortland grabbed her friend's hand. "You like him that much."

"No — yes — oh, I don't know. He gets to me."

Chuckling, Cortland shook her head. "My friend, you've got yourself a predicament."

CHAPTER NINE

The morning of the Fourth of July dawned bright and hot. The promise of clear skies through the evening made everyone planning fireworks displays ecstatic. Everyone except Andrew Kelly. It made him miserable. He knew what kind of day and night he was going to have thanks to those fireworks – busy.

Each Fourth of July or anytime there were fireworks displays, thousands of animals went out of their minds listening to the bangs and booms rattling the floors they lay on. It was the worst night of the entire year for animal control offices nationwide. Each year, hundreds of dogs broke loose from their owners and tried to flee the terrifying noise. And each year, Andrew received more calls for runaway and lost dogs on the Fourth of July than he received in most months.

If a dog didn't have a license tag, he'd try to find a chip implanted in the animal. If not, he'd try to match the dog to the descriptions of lost dogs called in that day. Sometimes it took him weeks to square everyone away although sometimes a dog remained lost and unaccounted for. It broke his heart to have to tell the owners there was nothing more he could do.

Andrew walked down the aisle of the kennels. All but two were empty. Inside, the building could hold eighteen dogs. If needed, he could house another twenty dogs outside. However, they would have to hear the roar of the fireworks. If he were lucky, it would be a quiet night, and it would be enough. But he wouldn't bet on it.

Walking back to his office, Andrew remembered this would be Hannah Woodbridge's first Fourth of July. He needed to call and give her a head's up about his likely need for her services. Sitting at his desk, Andrew dialed Hannah's vet office. It was several minutes before he was put through to her.

"Doctor Woodbridge, I will be needing your services tonight for sedation of a few animals, most likely."

"New dog having issues?" Hannah asked.

"No – it's the Fourth of July and tonight's the town's fireworks display. I always end up with a kennel full of anxious dogs. Sometimes forty or more. I should have warned you earlier. Hope you've got enough meds for that many, if needed."

Hannah breathed heavily, "Forty or more, are you kidding me?"

"Wish I was. That many could pass through my doors tonight."

"When does the fun begin? Should I just camp out at the shelter tonight?"

Andrew fingered the telephone cord on the old-fashioned desk phone, his mind racing in to perverse tangents at the thought of spending time alone with her. A part of his groin started to stiffen at the idea. He shook the thoughts away. "Fireworks display starts around nine. There will be some coming in all day thanks to backyard parties. Doc C. used to just hang out at the shelter. It was easier than making a dozen or more trips."

Both of them were quiet a few seconds. So much so that Andrew was afraid the line had gone dead. "Still there?"

"Yeah," Hannah replied. "I'll be over around eight. I'll bring some Sileo with me. If you need me sooner, skip the answering service and call me directly on my cell."

Andrew jotted it down as she rattled off the number. "Great, thanks," he said and hung up the phone.

By eight that night, he was down to five outside kennels unoccupied. People having yard parties had started early giving him an afternoon full of chasing lost dogs. So far, he had rounded up thirty-three dogs. Luckily, he'd been able to identify all, and their owners were on their way to the shelter. Considering the time it took for paperwork, Andrew issued citations they could mail in with their fines. He didn't have time to collect recovery fees today. Those that failed to pay their fines would find their dog's license held up for renewal.

Stomach growling, he sat in his chair watching the latest returned dog exit the front door. There hadn't been time for lunch and the way things were going, it didn't look like there would be time for supper either.

The office door opened, and Hannah Woodbridge walked in. "Hey, how's it going?" She scanned the room as if looking for evidence of disaster.

Rocking back in his chair, Andrew replied, "So far thirty-three dogs. Waiting for a few pickups before any more calls come in."

Hannah walked over to the kennel door and stared down the aisle. There was minimal barking coming from the holding room. "I'm on my way for a quick bite to eat. I thought I'd check in beforehand to see if you needed anything."

Still rocking, Andrew contemplated whether he should ask her to pick him up something to eat. On cue, his stomach growled in protest, making up his mind for him. "Would you mind picking something up for me?"

"No, not at all. I'm going to Roberto's."

Scribbling down his order on a notepad, he tore off the sheet and reached for his wallet. He pulled out a twenty-dollar bill and handed both to Hannah. "Any questions?"

She glanced at the note before saying, "Are you a vegetarian too?"

"Yeah," Andrew eyed her sheepishly. "You too?"

"Yes." She folded the note and stuffed it into her pants pocket. "I saw the movie on Temple Grandin as a kid. And I watched the documentary *The Ghosts in Our Machine*. They forever changed my thinking about the use of animals as a food and product source. How did you come to vegetarianism?"

"At Sinclair Community College I was a member of the vet tech club. We helped out at the puppy mill rescue in Shelby, Ohio. It was horrendous. Since then I have gravitated away from animal meat. It wasn't a singular decision. But I'm happy with it." Just remembering the puppy mill made Andrew's jaw clench tight. The experience had helped lead him eventually to his present job. Here he could do more as an ACO than he ever could as a vet technician.

They stared at each other a few moments, not knowing what else to say.

"I'll be right back." Hannah said and left as quickly as she had arrived.

Andrew watched her leave. Her walk had a little wiggle to it that snapped him to attention. All of him. *Whoa boy. Can't do that. No sense starting what can't be finished. What woman is going to want sterile goods?*

Four dog pickups and forty-two minutes later, the office door opened, and the smell of Italian food wafted inside along with Hannah Woodbridge.

Andrew swiped aside a mountain of paperwork on his desk. Taking the stack of bags out of her hands, he placed them on the cleared-off space. Hannah ripped open the top bag, digging out a Styrofoam container along with plastic utensils and napkins. She handed it to Andrew saying, "I think this one is yours," before digging into the second bag for a similar container.

Andrew pulled a chair beside the desk and motioned for Hannah to sit. They both sat down and began eating.

They were almost done with their meal when Andrew's office phone rang. He wiped his mouth and hands quickly before picking up the receiver. "Officer Kelly." He reached for the notepad, scribbling as he listened before hanging up the phone. "Sorry to leave you, but I have a call. Another runaway dog," he said. "It could be a while."

Hannah wiped her mouth and hands. "I'll stay here if you don't mind."

"No, not at all." Andrew said, closing his Styrofoam container before walking out the door.

For lack of anything better to do, Hannah cleaned up the supper mess. Spying a posterboard in the corner by the file cabinet that said "Adoption Fair Today," she picked it up. When Andrew was back, she turned the sign around and held it up. "What's this?"

Glancing up from his stack of papers, Andrew eyed it before returning to his work. "The Colby County Fair. It's coming up the second weekend in September. I have an adoption booth every year."

Hannah set the sign back down where she found it. "Do you get many adoptions?" Despite her question, her thoughts immediately went to the welfare of the animals. How well did they do amid the noise and crowds of a county fair? What if it was a hot day? Were they adequately sheltered and protected?

Not looking up as he wrote, he replied, "Some years I adopt everyone out. Other years, about half go that day, and few more later in the week. Why?"

She walked over to his desk and sat down in the chair beside it. "I'm curious about the conditions the animals might be in amongst the chaos. Do they do okay? Are they sheltered from the elements?"

Setting down his pen, Andrew glared at her. "Of course I manage their condition. Doc used to come by and check on them, informally, to make sure they were doing okay."

"So, I should be prepared to stop in?" Hannah cocked her head and waited.

Andrew sat back in his chair, his fingers playing along the length of the pen. "Yeah. Probably a good idea."

"And you were going to tell me about this when...?"

Frowning, he flung his hands wide, rolling his eyes. "It's only July 4th. Give me a break."

"I have patients booked for the next six months, every Saturday. I can't just bail on them to check on the adoption booth."

Raking a hand through his hair, he sighed. "I'm sorry. I never had to remind Doc. It was an oversight."

Appeased by his apology, she gave him a quick nod and then searched for her watch. Ten-thirty. "I'm going to bail on you now. If you think that's okay?"

He walked behind her as she hastened toward the door. "I should be okay. The backyard fireworks will continue until midnight no doubt, but most everyone with a dog will have secured it by now." He grasped her elbow before she stepped outside. "Where's Maggie tonight? How's she doing?"

Hannah's face broke into a wide smile. "My landlady, who also happens to be my next-door neighbor dog-sits her while I'm at work. She's elderly and alone, so she's thrilled to have Maggie's company during the day. Both are very happy with the arrangement. And I don't have to worry about either one of them." The warmth of his touch on her arm made her think of things she shouldn't be thinking of, not now, not ever, not with him. She moved her arm slightly and he withdrew his fingers.

He smiled too. "That's great to hear. I'm glad it's working out for all of you. But especially for Maggie Mae."

Hannah gave a nod then continued out the door. She glanced back at him from her car. He looked tired; his shoulders slumped; his posture bent. There was an aura of fatigue about him. How long he'd been working today she didn't know. Like her, there was no such thing as nine to five. Being on call twenty-four hours, seven days a week was exhausting but necessary. Her heart softened and her arms ached to cradle him in a warm, comforting embrace. *Nonsense. You can't touch him. Not even to comfort him. It might lead to —complications.* "Call me if you need me," she called across the parking lot before getting in the car and zooming away home.

CHAPTER TEN

The next morning Hannah was met at her office door by the practice manager, Barbra Pari. "I need to have a word with you."

The pretty middle-aged woman's smile was tense, her lips flat and thin.

Oh boy, what did I do now? "Sure thing. Just let me set my things down. Your office or mine?"

"Let's make it mine," Barbra said.

Hannah felt her breath catch. *Is Barbra handing in her resignation?*

After hanging her purse in her office closet, she set her lunch bag on her desk. It contained a peanut butter and jelly sandwich, and a banana. Hannah would have to eat in her office because of her sandwich. One of her veterinary technicians had a peanut butter allergy so eating with the crew in the lunch room was out of the question today.

She grabbed her white coat off the hanger in the closet and put it on. Taking the stethoscope out of the pocket, she slung it around the back of her neck. Her nerves steady at last, she headed to Barbra Pari's office.

Walking into the practice manager's office was like walking into a jungle. The woman not only loved animals, she loved plants and had two green thumbs to prove it. The windowsill of her office was covered with plants of all shapes and varieties. Not an inch of sill was free for another pot. Even areas of the floor space were covered by large pots of plants. A Norfolk pine in one corner, a four-foot-tall jade plant in another. The only surface that didn't have plants was her desk and that was only because there wasn't any room for a single potted plant. Stacks of papers lined the sides on the left and right edges while a computer screen took up space in the center of the desk. Her keyboard sat on the edge closest to her, surrounded by papers, pens, a few coffee mugs, and a stapler.

"Here I am," Hannah said, breezing through the doorway.

Barbra Pari's head rose up from her computer screen. "Shut the door please."

Hannah stopped short, wrinkling her nose but did as she was asked. "What's going on?"

"Have a seat," Barbra said, motioning to a chair before her desk. "I want to give you an update on a few issues we're having."

A loud sigh escaped Hannah's lips. "Is that all? My God, you had me worried there for a minute."

"Just wait until I tell you what's been happening, then you can decide whether to be worried or not."

"Okay, what's happening?" Hannah's gut quivered.

"I've been having to set aside one of the office staff to make photocopies every day. Photocopies of client files. Some of our clients are jumping ship."

The bottom of Hannah's stomach dropped. "How many?"

"Enough that I'm getting worried. About five percent of the practice has left. I know that doesn't seem like a lot, but it is."

"I don't feel any less busy during the day. No slack times, anyway," Hannah said.

"True. Business has been steady. I worry what the winter will be like. Most of our clients have their pets seen for annual physicals during the spring, summer, and fall, plus it's the bulk of our emergencies. Winters are usually light on injury and emergency cases."

"Is there anything we can do to deter it?" Hannah asked.

"Nothing I can think of. I would recommend we start instituting a charge for copying the client files. I've had Melissa on photocopying now for three days straight. It's costing us a small fortune in paper and copier fees."

Hannah thought for a minute. "No, no fees. I'd rather give it away than have them leave without any information on their pet." She thought for a moment. "Any idea where they are all going? There aren't many vets around this area."

Barbra snorted. "Yeah, they're all heading over to Bryan Plat's office in Wilkesbury.

"Bryan Plat, I've heard of him." He seemed to be having a significant impact on her career. Hopefully, he and this turn of events would not be having a significant impact on her ability to get the contract renewed.

"Nice guy. About thirty-five-ish, married, with a kid. He owns the only practice in the next town over. His wife is Andrew Kelly's sister."

Hannah reeled back in her chair, her mind swirling. *So that's it. Andrew wants his brother-in-law to get the bid. Now it makes sense. It's a family thing.* Why hadn't he told her about the connection? "Anything else?" Hannah glanced at her watch.

"Yeah, a ward tech and a vet assistant have given notice."

Hannah's gut sank. "Two? Were they worried about job stability?" She tried not to take the resignations personally, but coming so soon after taking over the practice, it was difficult.

"Maybe. They were weaseled away by Dr. Plat." Barbra crossed her arms over her chest and sat back in her chair. "Just as well. It makes our financial situation easier. And it eased the concerns of the remaining five staff members, even if it does make more work for them. Besides, we were a little heavy on staffing. Doc liked it that way."

Hannah nodded slowly.

Barbra crossed her arms over her chest. "Shall I start replacing them or wait?"

Hannah stood up and walked to the plant-filled windowsills. " I need to get some backup coverage. I can't be working 24/7/365. How did Doctor Cambria ever do it, at his age?"

Barbra smiled. "His wife was a huge help. She wasn't a vet, but folks who came here respected her help. And times were different way back when he started too. But as the attitudes changed, he did to. But he knew it was getting to be too much. Which is why he hired you." She gave Hannah a wink.

"Well, with the money saved from those two positions, can we support a part-time vet covering weekends and holidays and hire a replacement vet tech?"

Barbra pursed her lips. "It'll be tight, but I think we can swing it as long as no benefits are involved for the vet."

Hannah ran her thumb over a smooth jade leaf. The smell of wet potting soil and vegetation filled her nostrils. "I have a couple of classmates that haven't found full-time positions yet. One might bite at a part-time job."

"Anyone in particular in mind?"

"As a matter of fact —" Hannah smiled as she headed out the door.

Hannah called her former roommate, her nerves twitching as she paced the confines of her office. When the phone was answered, she said, "Hey, Cort, how are you?"

"Hannah! My God! I'm good. Are you doing any better?" Cortland Stewart seemed genuinely surprised to hear from her so soon after their dinner together.

"Let me tell you, girlfriend, it's worse. Everything has changed." Staring out the window, Hannah noticed someone had placed a flowering plant on her windowsill. Had to have been Barbra. She sniffed at the closest pink blossom. Lovely fragrance.

"What happened now?" Cortland asked, before adding, "Are you okay?"

"Yeah, I'm okay." She filled her best friend in on the changes that had transpired since their last conversation.

"So you really are the chief head honcho now?"

"Yeah, and it's killing me. I'm on 24/7/365 with no help. How about you? Did you find a job yet?"

"Negative. Not one I'm willing to move thousands of miles to some backwater place and make peanuts at anyway." She sighed. "So, I'm not really trying too hard just yet. The few interviews I had were pitiful. Then I thought, you know, I've been going to school for the last twenty years straight. I'm taking a little time off before I leap into the workforce for the rest of my life."

Hannah's heart sagged. "Yeah. Makes sense." It was advantageous that Cortland's parents could afford to keep supporting her. Both parents worked as doctors in the University of Rochester Medical System, her mom as an ob/gyn and her father as a urologist.

Hannah had never taken a break. Never considered it. But then her family circumstances weren't as stable as Cortland's. Her father's job didn't survive the bankruptcy at the Eastman Kodak Company. Unable to find another job, James had spiraled into clinical depression. Her mother, Dina, worked part-time as a bookkeeper at the local church.

Cortland mused, "Next time you come home, you should call me. Perkins isn't that far from Rochester."

Sighing aloud, Hannah replied, "Not likely, until I get some help here." And probably not even then unless hell froze over. She loved her parents, and her brother, Luke, but they had all sunken into depression. They functioned on a day-to-day basis amid the pall. Going home was like entering a funeral home. Somber, weighty, drowning. Hannah, having escaped, hadn't been home since leaving for her undergraduate degree, nearly nine years ago.

"Which is why I'm calling." Hannah added, forcing a smile to add a lift to her voice.

"Go on. What's the plan?"

"First order of business is to hire a part-time vet to cover weekends and share holidays."

"Part-time?"

"Yeah. Can I interest you in that?" Hannah crossed her fingers and her toes.

"Just weekends?"

"Maybe alternating holidays?" Hannah cringed. She didn't want to push it too far and make the job undesirable. Having Cortland with her would be better than great. She was someone Hannah could trust with her patients from the get-go. "I can't promise you benefits now. Or that it will turn full-time, but the possibility is there. It might take some time."

There was a moment of silence.

Cortland broke her silence. "Part-time working with you?"

Hannah added, "You can stay with me. You can sleep on the couch."

"Thanks. Daddy will be more than happy put me up in an apartment somewhere for a while, so long as I'm working." She hesitated again, then said, "One thing. I have a family wedding to go to Labor Day weekend."

"Fine. I can cover that weekend."

Giggling, Cortland said, "Okay then, I'm in."

Breathing a huge gush of relief, Hannah felt the weight of the world lift off her shoulders. "Awesome!"

"By the way —" Cortland asked, "What's your second order of business?"

"Winning the bid for town veterinarian."

CHAPTER ELEVEN

Valerie stuck her head in the door. Hannah looked up and stopped pulling off her white doctor's coat. "Hold on. You can't leave yet. The ACO's on his way with an injured raptor. ETA ten minutes. I'll put them in room one."

With a sigh, she struggled back into her coat. *Damn. Too bad Cortland left for the day already. She could have met Andrew. And dealt with the hawk. On the other hand, I get to talk with Andrew alone. Maybe settle some turbulence between us.* She tucked her stethoscope and penlight back in her coat pockets before heading out of the office.

Walking into room one together, she and Valerie found Andrew standing beside a blanket-covered carrier on the exam table. His work clothes were covered in dirt. A smudge of dirt on his cheek, and his tousled hair added to his rugged looks. Capturing the bird must have been difficult. Hannah felt a swell of admiration fill her chest for the man who looked after his charges so diligently. Spotting her, he looked up from his cell phone, then quickly stuffed it in his back pocket.

"Hello, Officer Kelly." Hannah approached the opposite side of the table. "What did you bring me today?" Valerie stood behind her ready to assist.

Andrew brushed his hand over his hair and smiled rather sheepishly. "Red-tail hawk, found alongside the road. Probably hit as it tried to fly across the roadway. It's right wing is a little mangled. Possible fracture."

Giving him a nod, Hannah turned and nodded to Valerie as well. "Okay, let's have a look."

Valerie assisted Andrew by removing the blanket, and then unlatching the top of the carrier while he grabbed a hold of the raptor with leather-gloved hands. The bird screeched its dissatisfaction at the disruption.

BID TO LOVE

Andrew held the raptor close to his chest, the injured side away from him while Hannah examined the wing as best she could; trying not to exacerbate the injury. "Hmm, I see what you mean. I think you're right. Let me give it a thorough exam, though."

Ten minutes later, she concluded, "I don't see or feel any other injuries. Which is surprising if she was hit by a car."

"That's good news." He answered, struggling to hold onto the wriggling bird.

"Can you carry her into the back to our cage? Valerie can show you the way." Hannah asked, stroking the soft feathered head of the avian, being careful to stay clear of the sharp beak.

The two disappeared into the animal holding areas of the clinic. Hannah typed her findings into the laptop computer on the countertop. In a few minutes, Andrew returned alone.

Hannah and Andrew looked at each other across the small room. A room Hannah felt was getting smaller and smaller by the minute.

"They told me you were leaving for the day. Thanks for staying late to look at the hawk," Andrew said as he reached for the top of his carrier.

Watching him re-connect the top to its base, her hands stuffed in her pockets, she nodded. "No problem. I wish Doctor Stewart were here to meet you and see the raptor."

He crossed his arms over his chest, a pinched expression on his face, and his eyes narrowing. "Doctor Stewart?" The tone of his voice revealing a hint of jealousy.

Hannah bit her upper lip, trying not to giggle. "Yes, I have hired a part-time veterinarian to cover weekends and alternating holidays. Doctor Cortland Stewart."

"Oh." The daggers in his eyes disappeared and his stance relaxed. "Good for you. No more seven days a week." He picked the blanket up off the floor.

Hannah reached out, grasping one end of the blanket as he stood up. "Initially, I'll have to ease her in to our system here. But eventually, she'll be on her own on the weekends." She stepped back holding a corner of the blanket in each hand. Andrew did the same, stretching the blanket out between them. Andrew cocked his head and gave her a sexy smile.

Her heart thundered as her own lips curved into a smile. *Covered in dirt, he's still the sexiest man I've ever met. And that smile is setting off fireworks all over my body.*

He raised an eyebrow and began approaching her. Hannah thought folding a blanket had never felt so ... erotic.

He stopped when they stood toe to toe. Simultaneously, they reached out, Hannah's fingers brushed his as she tried to take his corners from him. But he didn't let go. He covered her own fingers with his and held on.

Neither of them stepped back. Neither of them moved. She stared into his soft dark brown eyes, feeling her heart pounding in her chest so hard she could swear he heard every beat. His long brown eyelashes flickered, then his eyelids closed as his mouth grazed her own. The gentle brush of his lips sent her heart skittering and her breath stilled. *Holy smokes! What a kiss!* The zing of the contact sizzled throughout her body, leaving her wanting more. She bent forward, her lips searching for more.

At the rattle of the doorknob behind them they jerked apart.

"I—I'm sorry. I didn't think anyone was in here." Valerie stuttered, her eyes wide and twinkling, a grin fighting its way across her face. She backed out the door, closing it behind her.

"It's — um. He was just leaving," Hannah called out, her thoughts muddled, her cheeks on fire. She released her hold on the blanket.

Andrew finished folding it, grabbed his carrier and started to exit the room. Halfway out the door, with a silly grin on his face, he said "Thanks."

BID TO LOVE

***

Cortland flopped down on Hannah's office couch, threw her head back and closed her eyes. "Wow, this is worse than your couch at home." She smirked. "I didn't think that was possible."

"Very funny." Hannah deadpanned before breaking into a smile. "So, what do you think? You've been here all week getting the lowdown." Hannah rocked in her office chair, amused that her BFF was wiped out after five days of assisting. She remembered the fatigue she had felt during her first few weeks on the job, covering for Doc Cambria. More than once, she'd closed her eyes for a minute and fallen asleep on that very couch, only to be awoken to see yet another patient.

"I'm so glad it's going to be part-time. Maybe I'm not cut out for full-time employment." Cortland replied, her eyes still closed, head lolled back against the cushion. "But it's been great. The techs know their stuff, anticipate our needs. And the facility is clean and well organized."

Giggling at her friend, Hannah explained, "I can't take credit for any of it. Doctor Cambria built up the practice. He did a consummate job hiring good people. The ship runs smooth. With or without me."

Hannah's intercom crackled. "Dr. Woodbridge, Officer Kelly is here to see you."

Setting her chair upright, Hannah answered, "Send him down to my office." She turned to Cortland. "Look sharp, the town's animal control officer is on his way. This is good. You can meet him."

"Is he hot?" Cortland rose and straightened her clothes, smoothing out wrinkles in her pants and white lab coat, then running her fingers through her hair.

Heat swarmed Hannah's face. "Yes, I'd say."

Cortland, who had seen Hannah blushing, teased, "Ah, so there's something going on?"

"Shh!" Hannah hissed; her index finger planted before her lips.

A moment later Andrew rapped on the door frame, before pushing the door open and stepping over the threshold. He appeared startled to see someone with Hannah. "Sorry, I didn't know you were busy. I can come back later."

Hannah advanced toward him. "No, I'd like you to meet my new associate veterinarian, Doctor Cortland Stewart."

Andrew and Cortland shook hands.

"A pleasure," he said to Cortland, who blushed pink. "Another full-timer at the clinic?"

"No, part-time. Weekends and holidays," Cortland said before adding, "Sick days and vacation days too."

Andrew stuck his hands in his front pants pockets. "Congratulations. Also from Cornell?"

"Yup, classmates." Cortland stepped back, allowing Hannah more room to enter the conversation.

"And roommates," Hannah added.

Nodding, Andrew lapsed into silence, glancing between the two women.

After half a minute of this, Hannah asked, "Did you need to see me about something?"

Rocking on the balls of his feet, Andrew nodded. "Oh, yeah. I wanted to inquire about that red-tailed hawk I brought in two days ago."

Hannah walked back to her chair and sat down. "She went off to the rehabilitator in Butler County. Mid-shaft oblique fracture of the proximal right humerus. The animal hospital affiliated with the rehab facility performed the surgery."

"Good prognosis?"

"It should be able to be released after rehab. Assuming all goes well."

"Hit by a car?" Cortland asked, sitting down on the edge of the couch.

"Yeah, we think so. It was found on the side of the road," Andrew said. "Good news. The prognosis, I mean."

Cortland turned to Hannah. "You don't do avian surgeries?"

"Not on wildlife. The rehab places prefer to have their own affiliates do them."

Nodding, Cortland agreed. "Good to know."

"Whelp, I'll be heading out. Thanks for the update." Andrew gave Hannah a lingering look before turning to leave. He gave Doctor Stewart a nod. "Nice to meet you."

Cortland must have spotted the look between Hannah and Andrew. Jumping up, she headed for the door, passing Andrew. "I have to go check on our surgery patient." She disappeared out the doorway, closing the door behind her solidly as she left.

"Dr. Stewart seems nice." Andrew strode over to Hannah's desk. He sat down on the corner. "Great idea, getting your weekends free."

"Not initially. It will be both of us for a few weeks. Then I'll cut her loose on her own."

"And then, maybe…" His eyes bore into hers silently for some time. "Maybe you can get out more. For pleasure, I mean."

The hint of a smile grew across Hannah's face. "We'll see." A swarm of butterflies fluttered in her stomach at his innuendo.

Thirty minutes later, Cortland re-joined Hannah in her office. "Well, Kelly's one fine man flesh to look at." She flopped down on the couch again and grinned widely up at her friend.

Hannah rolled her eyes. "Okay, he's not hard to look at. But I can't get involved."

A puzzled look scrunched Cortland's face. "Why not?"

"Don't you remember what happened the last time I took up with someone I worked with? It ended up being a disaster. I nearly got fired." Hannah sighed.

"Bruce was trouble from the get-go. You were—."

"Too stupid to stay away. He was charming and funny and handsome." Hannah cradled her head in her hands. "Andrew's charming and handsome, and funny when he wants to be too. I can't go there again. Especially when I have this bid coming up. A bid I have to win. What if he has a say in the selection process?"

"Maybe that's all the more reason to, well, befriend him," Cortland suggested.

Hannah's mouth dropped open at her friend's idea. "I can't do that. You know that's not how I operate."

Sighing, she slumped deeper into the couch. "I know. You're right. Forget I even suggested it."

Silence surrounded the two women.

Cortland tapped her index finger against her curved lips a moment before saying, "Mind if I have a go? If you aren't interested, that is."

A flash of anger in her gut, Hannah crossed her arms over her chest. The hair on the nape of her neck stood up as she thought of Cortland and Andrew flirting and dating. The wiggling flame rose to her chest, settling in her heart. No, she didn't want to see the two of them together. She wanted...she wasn't sure. *What if he does have a say in the bid selection? Should I...*

"Earth to Hannah." Cortland whispered.

She looked over at her friend. More than anything she wanted to be able to say, "go for it." But the words could not form in her throat. An image of herself on his arm blossomed in her mind. But just as quickly the fear of what might happen again left her knees trembling. Could she, should she let herself try to have a relationship with Andrew Kelly? Experience told her it was too dangerous. Her one attempt at dating someone she worked with had gone horribly wrong. Her mental recriminations strongly advised her to not pursue another such relationship. No matter what.

But he's so handsome and you are both so much alike. Hannah's heart softened at the idea thinking of all the special moments they had shared: working over the fourth of July, adopting Maggie, that exquisite kiss just two days ago. Hannah's knees went weak just thinking of that kiss. *Why wouldn't it work?*

Cortland rose from the couch and stood before her, her eyes dark with concern. "Hannah? Are you all right?"

Placing her hand on Cortland's shoulder., Hannah finally replied. "Yeah, I do mind."

CHAPTER TWELVE

The cell phone beside him rang while he was on his way back to the shelter. The caller ID said "Kimberly." Andrew's gut clenched. *This can't be anything good.* He punched the call button. "Hey Kim. How are you feeling?"

A loud, sharp voice blasted through his phone. He jerked the phone away from his ear. "Brother of mine. I'm fat but fine. What are you doing next Saturday afternoon?"

"Hello to you too. Why? What's so particular about next Saturday?" He didn't bother trying to keep the furtive edge out of his voice.

"Why? Because it's your godson's birthday and I'm throwing a party for him. That's why." She sighed. "He's going to be four, in case you can't remember that either."

Scrunching his eyes, he rubbed his face with his palm. *How could I have forgotten?* "How is Daniel?"

"Excited to be having a party. He wants you there and so do I."

"I'll try to arrange coverage." Pulling his notepad out of his pocket, he scribbled down the date and Daniel Bday Party, underlining it several times.

"Excellent, and he's looking for some new superheroes Legos thingy." She went on. "Don't ask me for details. I know nothing about it beyond that. Ask Bryan."

"Right — Have Bryan give me a call. I'll see what I can do." He shoved the notepad and pen back into his pocket.

"It's only a week away now. Don't forget."

Trying to deflect, he asked, "Is he excited about a new brother or sister coming soon?"

"Yeah, he's hoping for a brother, of course. As is Bryan. I'm hoping for a girl."

Consider yourself lucky you can have either.

BID TO LOVE

Andrew's radio squawked. The dispatch wasn't for him, but Kim didn't know that. "Hey Kim, got to go."

"Don't forget Daniel," she drilled.

As if he could forget him. Bryan and Kim's first born had been named after his grandfather, Andrew and Kim's father, who had died of lung cancer six weeks before his birth. Andrew still got a hollow ache in his chest when the name came up. Realizing it was Daniel's birthday meant it was time for his yearly pilgrimage to the cemetery. "I won't forget."

"And bring a date, if you like."

A vision of Hannah, as she had looked when he met her — her white halter top soaked through with water — filled his senses making his knees feel weak. *Should I ask her?* He'd like her to meet his family. It felt important. Down to his toes. Then he had a vision of Hannah and Bryan circling each other like rival wolves over a carcass. *No, not going to bring Hannah. Not this time.* His heart fell at the prospect of not ever being able to bring her to meet his family. Especially if either she or Bryan got the town vet bid. His jaw tightened. Maybe he should be rooting for someone else.

***

The birthday party was in full swing by the time Andrew arrived.

"You're late." Kimberly air-kissed him since she couldn't reach over her baby belly to meet his cheek. She took the present out of his hands and placed it on the gift table.

"Sorry, I'm on duty. No coverage available today." He shrugged.

Kimberly gave him an open-mouthed, you-have-got-to-be-kidding glare across the space. "I told you a week ago."

"Well, it's summer and people go on vacation." He didn't bother to tell her, not only was he covering Colby, but he was covering Wilkesbury because their ACO was out of state for a funeral.

"Bryan's over by the pinata. Beer is in the cooler by the gas grill." She flung the sentences over her shoulder as a toddler led her away by the hand demanding a potty visit.

Surveying the backyard, Andrew spotted Bryan under the largest tree. He appeared to be arguing with Daniel who held a stick beneath a Spiderman pinata. He walked over to investigate and wish his godson a happy birthday.

Daniel's eyes pleaded with him, tears running down his chubby little cheeks, his blue eyes swimming with more tears. Sobbing, he grasped Andrew's pant leg and buried his face in the khaki fabric.

"Hey, pal, what's all this about?" He knelt down and gathered Daniel into his arms and tried to soothe him.

"I can't 'it 'im." Daniel wailed.

Andrew glanced up at Bryan, and mouthed "What?"

Bryan rolled his eyes. "He won't hit his Spiderman pinata." He bent over to his son's ear. "I'll do it for you, if you want."

Daniel shrieked, "NO! Don't hurt him!"

Bryan straightened, throwing his hands in the air. "Leave it to Kim to get the kid a pinata he can't destroy." He walked away cursing under his breath.

Andrew pushed Daniel away far enough to have a talk with him. Their eyes met. He was perfectly named, his godson. He somehow got his grandfather's eyes. Andrew liked to think his own son would have looked just like Daniel. Blinking back the seeds of his own tears, he said, "You know, Daniel, that Spiderman is a pinata. It's made of paper and it's full of candy."

Little Daniel nodded, his tears slowing though he still sniffled.

"And it's for a game. Whoever breaks the pinata open and spills all the candy out wins the game." Andrew smoothed his palm over Daniel's hair. The boy even had the same cowlick he did. Who knew it was a genetic trait?

"I don't want to break him." Daniel's voice cracked and new tears threatened to spill.

Thinking for a moment, Andrew said. "I have an idea. What do you say, I cut a little hole in the bottom of Spiderman's boot so we can get the candy out? Then I can tape the hole shut and you can keep Spiderman forever."

Daniel's face brightened. "Can you do it?" He rubbed at his eyes, making them redder.

"You bet, pal."

Taking his pocket knife out, he walked over to the pinata and cut it down. The surrounding kids all voiced their disappointment. "Don't worry, Daniel will share."

He turned to Daniel. "Hold out the bottom of your shirt." The little guy did as he was asked while Andrew slit a hole in Spiderman's boot and tipped out the candy into Daniel's shirttail. The kids started jumping up and down, anxious to get at the bounty. Daniel peered up at his godfather, amazement in his eyes.

"Go on and share the candy with your friends." Andrew gave his shoulder a little push toward the crowd of children. Daniel walked off, all smiles, into the throng.

Kimberly duck-walked up beside him. She took Spiderman out of his hands. "Good work."

"He has Dad's eyes."

"Yup." She wiped her eyes. "And your cowlick. Don't ask me how that happened."

He wrapped an arm around her shoulder as they strolled slowly toward the picnic table.

"You should have some of your own."

"What? Kids?" He stepped back to look at her, hesitating. *Tell her, damn it. So you don't have to listen to her harp on your love life all the time.*

"Yeah, kids." She bumped into his side as they resumed their walk back to the picnic table and cake. "You're a natural."

"Do you remember when I had surgery as a little tike, maybe first grade I think?"

Kimberly cocked her head while staring at him. "Yeah, sort of. I don't remember what it was about. I remember being miffed you got to stay out of school a long time."

He leaned closer and dropped his voice. "I had groin surgery." He looked her in the eyes. "And it's left me sterile."

Her eyes widened as her hand grasp his forearm. "Oh my God, Andrew. I didn't know! I'm so sorry!"

"It's okay. Just, please quit with the kid talk. Let me find the right woman first." As he said it his mind veered to Hannah. He shook his head to dispel the image. She had a maternal comfort around her. Like every other woman he knew, she would want children when she married. "Besides, I still have too much to do. I have to finish paying back Bryan for college tuition."

"Just help him get the town vet job and all is forgiven," Kimberly stared him in the eyes.

Andrew stopped in his tracks. "Are you serious?"

"Of course I'm serious. If he can get that job, we'll have enough money to take that cruise. And you can forget about repaying the tuition."

"You realize I don't have any pull with the selection committee. None whatsoever."

Kimberly leaned in a little closer and lowered her voice. "I'm sure there must be something you can do."

Andrew drew back and glared at her. "There's nothing I can do to influence the appointment. If Bryan gets it, it will entirely be by serendipity." He strode off to grab a slice of cake. Minutes later he had an animal control complaint call and left without another word.

CHAPTER THIRTEEN

Hannah put the last of the six kittens back into the cage with their mother. All had been checked and found to be in good health despite having been found in a damp, abandoned building earlier in the day. Momma cat licked the head and face of her returned offspring just before the kitten nuzzled its way down to her belly for a drink.

"Anything else?" Hannah called out to Andrew.

Andrew's gaze rose up from his paperwork. "Yeah, the spaniel cross in kennel two may have an ear infection, possibly both ears."

"Okay," she said, stuffing her instruments back into her black bag. She walked out of the cat room and headed for the kennel room. A blast of dog barks flooded the office area when Hannah opened the door. Hannah evaluated the spaniel, noting the infections in both ears as Andrew had predicted. She gave the dog a pat and belly rub before leaving him in his kennel.

Walking out of the kennel area, she re-entered the office. "You were right. Both ears are infected. Do you need Zymox or do you have some on hand?"

"I have some in the medicine cabinet, I think," Andrew said, turning his chair around to face the locked metal cabinet against the wall behind his desk. He pulled out his keys and opened the cabinet. "Yup, all set here. I think I have enough."

"Excellent, you know the instructions, right? Instill some into each ear and massage in, once daily for ten days. If it doesn't look cleared, continue the med for another four days. That should do the trick."

Andrew set the bottle of Zymox on the desk in front of him and relocked the cabinet.

Hannah sat down in a chair in front of the desk, splaying her legs. If there had been a foot stool or if it were her desk, she would have propped her feet up on it. They were aching pretty bad tonight. She had been on her feet since an emergency call at 5:30 in the morning. She pulled out her iPad and began making notes on the patients she had seen along with the conditions and treatments recommended.

As Andrew finished his paperwork, the phone rang again. He quickly picked up, once again reaching for the notepad. This time, however, he set it down immediately and hung up the phone less than thirty seconds later.

"Grab your bag. Let's go," he said, snatching the keys off his desk and heading for the door like the fire alarm had just sounded.

Hannah grabbed her bag and followed, skipping every other step to keep up with Andrew. "What's happening?" Hannah demanded.

Unable to answer as he climbed behind the wheel of the van, Andrew waited, the vehicle already running as Hannah climbed into the passenger seat.

"Old man Malin's on a bender. I have to go check on his dog, Toby."

Hannah struggled to buckle her seatbelt as the van bumped out of the parking lot onto the main road. Once secured, Hannah inquired, her tone raised, "Your phone call was the police telling you Mr. Malin was drinking?"

"No, that was Suzanne at the bar he frequents calling to tell me he's plastered and has been there all day."

"Why did she call you?"

Andrew looked over at Hannah a brief second and smiled, before going back to concentrating on driving. "She's part of my early warning system with Malin. She's one of many who have agreed to let me know when Malin's acting up again."

"Why?"

"Because he's more likely to abuse his dog when he's drunk."

Hannah stared out the window at the houses flashing by. "I can't believe you have this guy so steadily watched."

"If you had seen the condition of his last dogs when they were seized from him, you would understand."

BID TO LOVE

One hand clenching the dashboard, the other firm on the seat edge, Hannah hung on tightly as they sped down the dirt road. Careening over several substantial bumps, items in the back of the van crashed to the floor. Andrew and Hannah looked at each other; Hannah's eyes wide with fear, while Andrew's were hard.

The animal control vehicle pulled up outside Malin's trailer fifteen minutes later. Myron Malin's beat up Chevy pickup truck sat beside the trailer like it too had been rotting there for years. A weak light peeked out the grimy windows, indicating Myron was at home.

"Shit, he beat us here." Andrew smacked the steering wheel with both hands.

Taking up his binoculars, Andrew focused on the area near the back bumper of the trailer. There, as he expected, crouched the thin figure of Toby, Malin's dog. Nowhere within sight were there any dishes or containers that might hold food or water.

Andrew held out the binoculars to Hannah for her to look for herself. She took them and looked, scanning the entire area, not knowing where she would find the dog.

"Look by the rear bumper of the trailer."

Hannah swung the binoculars to the spot, nodding when she found the dog. "Now what?"

Reaching for his flashlight, Andrew answered, "I need to ascertain if the animal truly doesn't have any water or food."

Hannah nodded. "I don't see any bowls. But I do see something that looks like a laceration on the dog's neck."

"What?" Andrew grabbed the binoculars out of her hands and peered through them. "Yup, I see it too. It looks fresh. All the more reason to seize the dog." He set the binoculars down. "I need you to come with me."

"Me? Why?" Hannah croaked.

"Because I want a witness to collaborate my story in court."

Staring at him, Hannah stilled for moment before reaching for the door handle. Then she stopped. "One question," she said. "What if it's true? What then?"

Reaching behind his seat, Andrew withdrew large bolt cutters. "Then I use these to free the dog and take him into possession."

"Just like that? Without a court order?" Hannah asked, her voice quavering. "Can't we just knock on the door and ask the man to hand him over for treatment?"

He looked at her askew. "No need. I already have the authority as Colby ACO and court permission. Remember, this is a repeat offender." His eyes locked on Hannah's. "Ready?"

Hannah gave him a dubious glare before reaching for the door handle again and giving it a push.

"Hold this," he said, handing her a leash.

The two of them walked toward the trailer as if on egg shells, Andrew carrying the fetch pole in one hand and bolt cutters in the other. Hannah hung back a step, trying to stay out of the way of the pole. They got within three feet of the rear bumper of the trailer before the dog started growling.

"Here, boy," Andrew said, reaching into his pocket and pulling out a handful of dog treats. He tossed them at the dog, who flinched and moved away. His nose caught the scent of the treats in a few seconds, and he lunged back for them, gobbling them up without tasting them.

Andrew took a few steps closer, holding out a handful of treats this time. Hannah held her breath as she watched the dog inch his way closer.

"Check for dog bowls again," Andrew said, nodding his head in the direction of the trailer.

Taking tentative steps, Hannah approached the trailer, her eyes scanning for bowls but there were none. "I still don't see any," she said.

"That's what I thought. So, if I can get Toby on a leash quietly, I will. Otherwise, I'll use the fetch pole. He's seen me before and we're old buddies, but hunger does strange things to an animal's mind. He might not recognize me."

Andrew knelt, his hand still out, filled with dog treats. Toby approached, coming closer, until he was within touching distance of Andrew's finger. The dog stretched his neck out, using his tongue to pull the treats out of Andrew's hand. Several treats dropped to the ground. Toby pounced toward them, snatching them up quickly. Andrew reached out with his palm forward. The dog sniffed his palm, then turned away without reaction. This time Andrew reached out and grabbed the dog's collar. His other hand, holding the leash, snapped the leash to the collar and unhooked the chain. "Come on, boy, let's get you some real food."

Toby responded to the slight tug on the leash by planting all four paws in the dirt and pulling back. Andrew pulled out another treat from his pocket. "Come on boy, no time to balk now. I'm running out of treats here. Let's get going."

Hannah picked up the fetch pole and bolt cutters and started for the van. She was halfway to it when the door to the trailer popped open and a disheveled elderly man stuck his head out the opening.

"What are you doing on my property?" he slurred, one arm flailing wildly while the other held on to the doorframe.

Hannah kept heading for the van, "Nothing sir, just leaving," she said, hoping he would not see Andrew and Toby, hidden from his view behind his open door. Both Andrew and Toby had stopped and shrunk back against the trailer to keep from being seen by the angry drunken man.

"Get going then. Get out of here."

Hannah sensed he wasn't going to go inside until she had gotten into the van and perhaps even left. She looked over to where Andrew crouched against the trailer. He mimed turning a steering wheel then waved down the road. Hannah got the impression he wanted her to drive off. If she did that, perhaps Mr. Malin would go back into his trailer and then she could come back around to pick them both up.

She got into the driver's seat, started it up and put it in drive. As it inched forward, out of the side mirror she could see Mr. Malin closing the trailer door. Andrew and the dog remained perfectly still. Once the van was a hundred feet down the road, and the trailer door completely closed, Hannah pulled over and with some effort managed to do a U-turn, heading back past the trailer.

When she got within twenty feet of the trailer, Andrew and the dog made a run for the roadway. As she stopped, the back door of the van was already open. Hannah could hear the claws of the dog scratching on the metal floor in the back. Andrew's voice came up from the back, "Give me a minute to get Toby secured, then let's get the hell out of here."

The clanking of the cage door told Hannah Toby was secured. She put on her seatbelt and reached for the gear shift.

Suddenly, the trailer door opened up again and Mr. Malin came stumbling out, his shirttails flying in the breeze, with a rifle in hand.

"Hang on! Time to go!" Hannah yelled, jamming her foot down on the gas pedal. The tires spun on the dirt road, kicking up a cloud of dust. As the van lurched forward, Hannah heard something land with a thud on the floor in the back. She hoped it was Andrew instead of Toby.

When she was a quarter mile away, she slowed down and stopped in the middle of the road. She got out of the driver's seat and peered through the little window into the back of the van. There, lying on his side, was Andrew, his hand to the back of his head. She yelled back to him, "Are you okay?"

Andrew looked up at the window. "I'm bleeding from the back of my head and it hurts like hell. Don't think it's serious. Let's get to the shelter."

Hannah's heart lurched. What had she done to him? There was no way she was going to wait until they were at the shelter before she checked out his head. She climbed back over the driver's seat and exited the vehicle. Opening the back door, she found Andrew sitting up beside Toby's cage. The dog looked fine, but Andrew's face was pale.

She grabbed him by the arm to turn him around. With the flashlight on, she pulled his hand away from the back of his head, revealing a mass of bloodied hair. Hannah picked the hair aside, strand by strand to reveal a gash. It still oozed blood but not nearly as much as it had previously. Hannah looked around. "You have a first aid kit in here somewhere?"

"Yeah, behind the driver's seat."

Hannah got the kit and opened a couple packages of gauze pads which she pressed against the laceration. "Here, hold this against your cut. You're going to need stitches."

"No stitches," Andrew said, taking over holding the gauze.

"Sorry, buddy. You need stitches."

Frowning, Andrew changed the subject. "Let's get Toby in the shelter first."

Andrew managed to walk to the passenger seat while Hannah returned to the driver's seat. They drove to the shelter in silence. Once there, Hannah could see from the definition of Toby's ribs, the poor dog had been without adequate food for a little now. His laceration was infected. She cleaned the wound quickly and gave Toby a shot of antibiotic. Fortunately, there weren't any obvious signs of abuse; though, she wouldn't see any internal injuries or healed broken bones without more extensive tests like x-rays. She would see him at the clinic in the morning for a more thorough evaluation.

"Now Toby's settled with food and water. Let's get you to the hospital for some stitches and maybe an x-ray." Hannah said.

"Do you really think it's necessary?" Andrew said. "I have a lot of paperwork to do for court about Toby and Mr. Malin."

"Yes, I'm sure you do. This time of night it should only take an hour or so in the ER. Come on, I'll drive you." She stood at the door, expectantly holding it open.

Andrew acquiesced, following Hannah out to her car, and getting in without complaint.

"Is it going to be difficult to get the court to agree to a surrender?" Hannah asked as they drove through the streets of Colby.

"I don't know." He rubbed the nape of his neck. "Judge Croft presided over the last episode with Myron Malin. He was the one who told me to just seize the dog next time and come back to him with the paperwork."

Were that it was that easy in every jurisdiction. The lives of many pets could be made better, sooner, instead of a long-drawn-out process allowing perpetrators more time to abuse and neglect animals.

"Hey, you don't have to stay at the ER with me. I know you're tired and it's well after midnight. I can get a ride back to the shelter from one of the police officers."

Hannah looked him over. It sounded good to her. She had office hours at eight in the morning. A few hours of sleep would be wonderful, and she still had to walk Maggie Mae. Her heart told her she couldn't abandon Andrew no matter what he said.

"Let's swing by my apartment. I'll let Maggie out for a few minutes; then, I'll take you over to Colby Hospital."

"If you're sure," Andrew said, his elbow sticking up in the air as he held the gauze to his head.

They drove to Hannah's apartment where Maggie Mae happily relieved herself quickly before being tucked back inside. Within minutes they were on their way to the emergency room. As they pulled in the driveway, Andrew said, "Just drop me off at the ER door."

Hannah shook her head. "Nothing doing, Kelly. I'm going in with you."

"Oh no, you're not. Go home. Get some sleep." Andrew said, his hand on the door handle.

"Thanks, no. We're partners in crime tonight. That includes the aftermath." Hannah said as she parked the car.

Andrew frowned at first, but a smile crept over his face. "I guess you've got a point there."

Reaching for the door handle, she caught his glance and froze in place. *Such beautiful eyes!*

He grasped her right hand and gave it a squeeze. "Thanks for everything. I couldn't have asked for a better accomplice."

Hannah felt the heat of a blush rising up her neck and face. "Ah, it was kind of fun. And we got to save Toby."

An ear-to-ear grin broke out on Andrew's face. "Yes, it was. I can say that now. And yes, we did get Toby. At long last."

They squeezed each other's hand. And with that, they went into the ER for what turned out to be thirteen stitches.

CHAPTER FOURTEEN

Her shoe heels clicked along the sidewalk at a swift pace, as Hannah rushed from her parked car. The Colby County Courthouse, her destination, sat between the opera house, where the local theatre group performed, and the post office. Across the street was the library, to the right of which was the police station, and on its left was an old school building repurposed as a senior center. The busy downtown traffic had forced her to park two blocks away in a municipal parking lot.

Like the old school and the library, the courthouse was made of red brick, with large, paned windows, two stories in height. Built during the Great Depression era, the concrete steps to the courthouse were flanked by green, oxidized copper statues of Lady Justice and Prudentia, the personification of virtue, created by the Civilian Conservation Corps artists. If she had her running shoes on, Hannah would have taken the steps two at a time. It wasn't possible in heels and she didn't want perspiration stains on her blouse from the heat and the stress of rushing. She approached the doors beside which were large urns filled to overflowing with wilting green foliage and drooping bright blossoms.

Slightly cooler inside, the institution-style corridors with linoleum floors and wood doors had hardly been updated since construction. Minor safety and handicap accessibility changes had been made, barely bringing the building up to code. The county did not wish to spend too much on the old building but needed to keep it in compliance for it to remain useful. Hannah had been in town long enough to know there was no funding available for a new courthouse building.

Hannah headed to courtroom number three for the proceedings of the Town of Colby vs Malin. As she entered from the corridor, she spotted Andrew already giving testimony. On tip-toes, she hastened to take a seat on the prosecution side of the courtroom. The presiding official, a withered, white-haired Judge Bertram Dobson, looked disinterested on his bench, frequently peering off into space or checking his fingernails.

"There weren't any food or water bowls in sight and a wound of some sort was visible on the dog's neck."

"How did you know this? Had you approached the animal?" the lawyer asked.

"Dr. Woodbridge and I were looking through binoculars at first from the road. When probable cause was established, I approached the dog to investigate further."

"And then what happened, Officer Kelly?"

"I ascertained that there were no food or water bowls, and that the dog did in fact have a wound on his neck. I released him from his chain and brought him to the Animal Control van."

"Did Mr. Malin have any reaction to this?"

"Yes. He came out the door of his trailer with a rifle in hand threatening us."

"He threatened you with a firearm?"

"Yes, sir." Andrew looked over at the judge, but he was reading a paper, oblivious to the testimony being given.

Andrew was dismissed. He walked down the courtroom aisle. Glancing up, he caught sight of Hannah and smiled before he took a seat at the prosecution's table.

Hannah knew she was likely to be called next. Butterflies fluttered in her stomach as she waited for her name to be called. She had never given testimony in a courtroom before, and she was terrified she would make a mistake that would cost Toby his freedom.

Just as she'd suspected, Hannah was called next and sworn in as a witness.

"Dr. Woodbridge, did you go with Officer Kelly to the home of Myron Malin?"

" I did." Hannah felt the fluttering subside as she delved into the answer to the question.

"Do you concur with the officer that there were no food or water bowls anywhere near the dog and that he had a wound of some sort on his neck."

"Yes, absolutely. I looked through the binoculars and didn't see any bowls and spotted the laceration."

"What was the condition of the dog after you had time to examine him?"

"My professional opinion is he was undernourished. Slightly underweight and the laceration on his neck was infected. His wound was cleaned thoroughly. Then I gave him medications for possible malnutrition and included antibiotics for the wound. And he was properly fed."

The prosecuting attorney had no further questions. The defense had no questions either, so she was dismissed. Walking back to her seat, Andrew caught her eye and winked. Her lips twitched as she nearly burst out laughing at the absurdity of the gesture in such a solemn place.

When the prosecution had no additional witnesses, the defense called Myron Malin to the stand for testimony. A spotless and orderly Mr. Malin strode to the stand, his neatly combed and slicked back hair not moving. Even his dress shirt was, if not ironed, at least wrinkle free and his jeans looked new. Hannah was surprised at the change in his appearance from the last time she had seen him; a rifle in hand, his tattered shirttails fluttering behind him, his hair sticking up on end. Clearly he had cleaned up his persona for today's event.

"Mr. Malin, Officer Kelly and Doctor Woodbridge have both testified there weren't any food or water bowls out for your dog, Toby. Can you explain why?"

Myron Malin sat up straight, his head at a cocky angle. "There weren't any bowls because I had just taken them in to wash and refill."

"Have you been feeding your dog, sir?"

He turned toward the judge. "Yes, of course. He's my pal. My buddy. He gets fed every day and he always has water."

The defense attorney, still standing before the witness stand, said, "One more question, Mr. Malin. Did you know about the wound on the dog's neck?"

"I had just seen it when I got his bowls a few minutes earlier. I was going to clean it up and bandage it after I brought out his food and water." He flashed a smug smile at the prosecution table.

Andrew whispered furiously at the prosecuting attorney, but he stood up and said he had no questions for Mr. Malin.

With both sides resting their case, it was the judge's turn to decide the fate of Toby. Judge Dobson took a brief recess in his chamber to deliberate on the testimony presented. During the recess, Andrew approached Hannah.

"How's your head?" Hannah asked, trying to peer at the spot on the back of Andrew's head where the stiches were located.

"It's fine. I get the stitches out tomorrow."

Hannah nodded and readjusted her purse in her hands. "How do you think it's going to go?"

Andrew shrugged. "If Judge Croft were here, I'd say it's a slam-dunk. I have never had a case before this judge." He cupped his hand alongside his mouth and got close to Hannah's ear. "Frankly, I don't know where they scrounged him up, but he looked like he couldn't care less about what was going on."

"Yeah, I noticed he wasn't paying much attention to what anyone was saying," Hannah whispered.

After thirty minutes, a rustling noise at the judge's bench and a call to order from the bailiff sent them both back to their seats.

Judge Dobson entered, stumbling as he stepped up to his bench and sat down.

"I have considered all the testimony given and have concluded that the prosecution has failed to convince me that the dog is in grave danger with his owner. That being said, Mr. Malin, you are reminded to feed and water your dog properly or you'll be back here again. This case is dismissed." And with that, the judge banged down his gavel.

It didn't feel right to just leave the courthouse and separate. They had fought the battle as a team and lost. Commiserating together felt right to Andrew, which was what he said when he offered to buy Hannah a drink.

Pascoe's Restaurant was set up in an old house built in the 1790s. Serving quality New England country fare, it prospered. An addition to the back of the house held the upscale bar with gleaming brass and oak everywhere. Despite the country antiques and old pictures hanging on the walls, the bar furnishings were contemporary, comfortable, and clean. The upper-class clientele kept the place filled as there wasn't another place with such quiet and subdued luxury for another ten miles.

Hannah stared out the window at the glowing sunset, lost in her thoughts. Her fingers played idly on the stem of her wineglass, the straw-colored liquid inside shimmering in the candlelight. She still could not believe the magistrate had ruled against the seizure. A wave of heat rolled up from her belly again at the thought of his words.

"That was a heavy sigh," Andrew said, carefully placing his pilsner glass on the glossy surface of the oak table. His face still registered shock at the judge's verdict. It was beyond disappointment.

Hannah looked up at him. "I can't imagine what the judge was thinking, sending that poor dog back to Mr. Malin. How much more is he going to suffer before we can convince a judge he needs to be removed from Malin's custody?"

Lips twisted with bitterness; Andrew shook his head. "Why did Judge Croft have to retire so soon? He assured me further neglect on the part of Malin would automatically qualify as cause for seizure. Judge Dobson either didn't get that memo or didn't care to recognize its validity." He sighed heavily. "Also, I didn't have the usual attorney with me in court. That wasn't the town's attorney. It was a back-up. The new guy didn't listen to my suggestions for questioning. A lot of potential damning testimony questions never got asked of Mr. Malin. They could have helped our case substantially. And he refused to call for Desmond's law advocates."

"Desmond's law?"

"Desmond's law allows Connecticut courts to appoint advocates in animal abuse and rights cases...someone who represents the interests of justice. They are a dedicated group of Connecticut University law students and pro-bono lawyers who assist counsel before and during court hearings. But this substitute lawyer couldn't be bothered to get them in on Toby's case."

It had been a long day, between seeing to the appointments at her practice and racing over to the courthouse to provide testimony midafternoon. Tears welled in her eyes as she felt the weight of the judge's decision on her shoulders. Maybe she hadn't told him enough. Maybe she should have described the physiological ramifications of dehydration and starvation on the dog and the types of diseases it could cause or exacerbate. Tears spilled down her cheeks. Hannah wiped them away quickly with the back of her hand, her eyes darting left and right to see who might have noticed.

"Hey, take it easy," Andrew said, laying his hand on her forearm. "It's going to be okay. A minor setback. That's all."

"It doesn't feel minor. Not to me and not to Toby, I'm sure. Didn't you notice how quickly and how much food he gobbled up while at the shelter? We should have brought pictures of him." Hannah had seen a lot of hungry dogs in her years in vet school, her internships at shelters, and with rescue groups. She had never seen a dog eat as readily and as quickly as Toby. The poor creature had been without food for more than a couple days. The prominence of his ribs under his skin also proved this condition was a chronic one. Despite Andrew's daily checks, the dog was not getting enough sustenance.

Andrew was silent a moment before nodding. Then he smiled. "The fight isn't over yet. I'm still going to be on Malin's case. Still going to check on his dog every day. Don't think that I won't."

Her tears continued to flow despite Andrew's pep talk. "Look, I have to get going," she said suddenly, downing the last inch of wine in her glass and getting up from her chair.

Andrew threw two twenties down on the table and got up with her. "Let me see you to your car," and he walked her out.

Outside, the night air blanketed them like flannel, warm and tactile with mist. The moisture brushed against Hannah's skin, causing a shiver down her spine. Or was it the handsome man walking beside her?

Hannah and Andrew walked to the Corolla in silence. Having reached the car together, they turned to one another. Andrew slumped against the hood; his eyes locked on hers. Hannah saw the pain there. Pain she recognized all too well. They both had lost today. There was no getting around that fact. The one who had really lost today was Toby. At the thought, a croak escaped her throat and Hannah let flow the tears she had held back for too long.

Startled, Andrew reached out to her. "Hey, don't cry. It's going to be okay." He took her hands in his, but it seemed inadequate. When her sobs continued unabated, he pulled her into his arms and tenderly rocked her side to side, letting her cry on his shoulder. All the while, he whispered in her ear how they would continue to watch after Toby and make sure he was being treated appropriately.

He rubbed his hand over her back, soothing her while she quaked with sobs. His body came to full attention, aware of her with every sense.

She quieted, still clinging to him, her chin resting on his shoulder. His arms still nestled around her, holding her close, Andrew breathed deeply, smelling the lovely, herbal fragrance of her hair. He reached up and stroked his hand down the long tresses, luxuriating in the silkiness.

Would her skin feel just as silky beneath his fingertips? Her body against him, her breasts pressed against his chest, he ached to explore their softness.

Her firm thighs pressed on either side of his leg. Heat began to ignite where they touched. Feeling himself stiffen, he turned his face into her neck. The velvety whiteness called to his lips, and he obeyed. Small kisses fell in a circle at the base of her ear and just behind it. Hannah inhaled and moaned softly into his shoulder, rolling her head aside to lay more of her neck bare. Andrew complied with her silent request, dropping slow, sweet kisses on her exposed neck. He pushed aside her hair, exposing the nape of her neck to lavish with his lips and tongue.

With a groan, Hannah raised her head, her eyes glowing. Andrew felt his heart throbbing in his chest. He leaned over and captured her lips with his own, gently at first, then with more pressure. Hannah responded, giving her lips over to his. When his tongue grazed the edge of her lip, Hannah's tongue sought out his. They played and teased until, breathless, they parted.

Hannah looked up at him, trembling, searching his eyes. Andrew found himself captured by their luminescence, unable to speak, afraid to speak. Afraid to break the spell they had fallen under. Heat raged in his body, he ached to take her in his arms again and crush her against him.

Clearing her throat, Hannah broke the spell, "I have a smooth bottle of Scotch at home."

Andrew felt his heart leap in his chest. "I'm right behind you," he said, pulling his keys out of his pocket.

"No, come with me. I don't need a big white animal control van sitting in my driveway, informing the world who I'm with," she said, taking his hand and giving it a squeeze.

Hannah followed him to the shelter where he left the van, getting into her car for the ride to her apartment.

***

Something crept over her sleepy senses spiderlike; slowly, tentatively but suspiciously eerie. The dual sounds of light breathing brought Hannah to wakefulness. One set of respirations came from Maggie on the floor beside her bed. Rolling toward the center of the bed onto her side she bumped into a body. A naked body. The other source of breathing now grunted and moaned. *Oh, sweet Jesus. I really did have sex with him last night. Stupid! Stupid! Stupid!* She slid back as far away as she could, pulling the sheet up over her bare breasts. Her eyes met Andrew's gorgeous eyes just as they opened.

"Good morning," he muttered, his eyes soft and sleepy. The lids fluttered shut again.

Hannah's mind spun remembering the night before. She closed her own eyes, her hand covering them.

"Are you okay?" His fingers touched her nearest shoulder. "Headache?"

Her body twitched at the touch of his fingers and her eyes flew open. And there was his sexy smile and her body started humming a happy tune. The same tune it hummed last night, several times in fact. "Umm —" Hannah cleared her throat. "I'm a little —" *What word to use?*

He rose up on one elbow, frowning. "What?" His eyes sparkled in the morning light. "A little what?"

She tugged the sheet up closer to her chin. "A little — uncomfortable."

He blinked several times, eyebrows raised. "Shall I leave?" He sat up, the sheet sliding down, revealing his perfectly formed chest. The same chest her tongue and lips had explored last night. "I can get an Uber so you don't have to drive me to the shelter." He flung back the covers to get out of bed.

Squeezing her eyes shut and rolling onto her back, Hannah pondered her options. Letting him get an Uber would certainly make life easier, but it wasn't very hospitable. *Not that I'm being hospitable now, I just don't know what to do.* This was the first time she had ever had an overnight guest. She had to do better. "No, it's okay. I'll drive you."

She stayed in bed, staring out the window, then at the dappled sunlight on the wall, listening as he got up and dressed. At the sound of a zipper, she sighed, releasing a breath she didn't know she was holding.

"I'm going to use your bathroom." Andrew called on his way down the short hallway to the one bathroom in the apartment.

Only then did she dare to open her eyes. "Sure thing. Should I, um, make some coffee?"

There was no reply. She leapt up and frantically rummaged in her bureau for clean underwear. Hopping as her toe caught on the lace edge, she struggled into fresh panties. Hands trembling, she wrestled her bra in place. But the hooks and eyes weren't cooperating. Fumbling, she started over, whispering curses.

"Want some help? Not only do I know how to take one off, I also know how to put one back on."

Heat flushed her face. Twisting around, she found Andrew leaning against the bedroom doorjamb watching her dress.

"No thanks, I'll get it." She closed her eyes and pleaded with herself to slow down. The bra cooperated and clasped. Sixty seconds later she was decked out in jeans, a t-shirt, and flip flops. Turning back around, she saw he had been watching her dress the entire time.

"Lovely. You are so beautiful." He smiled, a glint in his eyes and started her way. "Maybe we should repeat —"

"Never mind that." She slipped by him without touching him "Let's go."

The ride to the shelter was silent except for the persistent panting of Maggie over their shoulders from the back seat. They arrived at the shelter in record time. Hannah left the car running directly in front of the door.

Andrew rested his hand over Hannah's as it gripped the stick-shift of the car. "I want to thank you for last night. I hope you enjoyed it as much as I did." He gave her a sweet smile and leaned over, dropping a kiss her cheek.

The butterflies in Hannah's stomach lurched into orbit. *What can I say? If I say I enjoyed it, he might think I want it to happen again. And yet if I say I didn't, I will hurt him, and it wouldn't be the truth either.* "It was fun. Thanks," she said, her tone coming out more clipped and curt than she intended.

He sat back in his seat a few seconds, the sparkle in his eyes extinguished. "Okay." He reached for the door handle and started to exit the car.

Impulsively, Hannah grabbed his arm before he got too far. He sat back down. "I really mean it. Thank you."

Andrew's radio went off. He leaned over and gave her a kiss on the lips this time. "Have a good day," he said as he got out of the car. He walked to the shelter door answering the radio call.

Breathing a huge sigh of relief, Hannah pulled out of the parking lot as Maggie slipped between the seats, resuming her rightful place as co-pilot.

CHAPTER FIFTEEN

Three days after, Hannah still had not heard from Andrew. Based on his failure to follow through, she chalked up her evening escapade with him as a night to remember, but a one-time occurrence. After all, they were consenting adults. They had a fling. What more did she really have time for with such a busy veterinary practice? It was stupid they had even done it. Hannah shook her head to rid her mind of the images of a naked and spectacular looking Andrew Kelly.

"What's that?" her assistant, Valerie asked.

Feeling the fire of a blush crimson her face, Hannah cursed beneath her breath and muttered back, "Nothing. I was just thinking of something I forgot to do at home this morning."

She picked up the next client file and quickly skimmed the note. *Rule out lick granuloma, left rear hock, 3 days.*

The overhead speaker blared her name, "Doctor Woodbridge, line four, please. Urgent."

Moving to the nearest phone, she punched a button and answered, "Doctor Woodbridge."

"Doctor Woodbridge, it's Officer Kelly."

"Good morning, officer. What's the emergency?" Hannah said, her voice a little harsher than she would have liked. She hoped he wasn't using the emergency as a ploy to get a quick personal call through to her. She would have to chew him out if that was the case.

"We have a situation that may require your immediate assistance. There's a wild fire up on Colburn Ridge on the west side of town. It's gaining strength. May overrun the firebreak. We could have a number of wild animals injured as a result. Just wanted to put you on alert in case you're needed."

Hannah was speechless for a few seconds, digesting the information. A wild fire just outside of town. Her mind raced with the potential injuries: burns, dehydration, smoke inhalation, exhaustion from trying to outrun the flames, heat exhaustion, heat stroke.

"Thanks for the warning, I'll get my crew set up for a potential influx of patients."

"Thanks, Hannah. I knew I could count on you," Andrew said before hanging up.

Hannah hung up the receiver and called Barbra Pari. "Time to activate the mass casualty plan. Only this time it is not a drill. There's a wild fire on the west side of town. The ACO thinks we might be getting some wildlife. And call in Dr. Stewart if she's available."

***

Smoke billowed in the darkened western sky as the wildfire raged on the ground below. Firefighters with shovels and pickaxes hovered just in front of the fire line, tamping here, shoveling there, to smother the blossoming flames as they spread toward them. Two hundred yards back from the line, Andrew watched them through the shower of ash falling around him. Beyond the fire line he could see pockets of burning detritus and smoking debris. So far, the extent of injured animals had been few. One rabbit had hopped beyond the fire line, its fur singed in places. He had quickly snagged by Firefighter Dawson Michaels, who flagged down Andrew along the road.

"You think there'll be more? Should I stay or deliver this guy to the clinic?"

Dawson hitched back the brim of his helmet to wipe his sweating forehead. "It's almost out in this area. The other side might give you some business, but safe to say get this fella to the clinic."

"Right." Andrew said before securing the rabbit in a cage. He grabbed an armful of water bottle and handed them to Dawson. "Here. Looks like you guys could use these. Call me if you need me again."

The sun was a hazy glow in the smoke-filled sky. Andrew checked his watch. Three-thirty-four. It did look as though the fire was under control on this part of the line. Perhaps he would take a run into town with the rabbit, grab some take-out for a late lunch and maybe come back. He pulled out his keys and motioned he was leaving to the nearest firefighter. The firefighter nodded and waved her shovel before resuming her work on the line of fire inching toward her feet.

The ride to the vet clinic was uneventful. A low cloud of smoke hung over the town of Colby, giving the residents pause. Most stayed off the roads, sticking to their radios and televisions sets for warnings to evacuate should the fire line draw too close to their side of town.

Andrew pulled into the clinic. The parking lot was almost empty. A veterinary technician rushed to the back door of his van, offering to assist him in carrying any animals into the building. She seemed a little disappointed, and yet, relieved to see it was only the one rabbit in need of medical attention. Andrew let the technician transport the carrier into the clinic through the side door as he followed.

He was met by a team of veterinary technicians, Doctor Woodbridge, and Doctor Stewart, who all nearly pounced on the rabbit's crate as soon as it was inside. Realizing it was only one animal, everyone except Hannah and one vet tech backed out of the exam room.

"Officer Kelly," Hannah said, acknowledging his presence. "What do we have here?"

Andrew froze at the sight of Hannah. Her silky hair was hanging free, reminding him how wanton she'd looked riding him; her long hair spread over her breasts, nipples peeking out between the strands.

"Officer Kelly?" she repeated.

He roused, cleared the catch in his throat. "Ah, yeah, a rabbit. A little singed on one side. I don't think it's seriously hurt but a check-up couldn't hurt."

Terror shown in the rabbit's eyes as it was placed on the stainless-steel examination table.

Hannah stepped forward; stethoscope poised to listen to the animal's lungs for symptoms of smoke inhalation. A few minutes later, she examined its eyes and nostrils, and tried to examine its mouth, careful to avoid an encounter with its teeth. A look at the singed fur and body, and she stepped back away from the table. With a nod, a technician picked up the rabbit and replaced it inside the carrier.

"Seems okay. No signs or symptoms of smoke inhalation. The fire merely singed the fur. No skin or other body parts appear affected."

Andrew nodded. "Excellent," he said. "I can take it back to the shelter for now and release it later when the fire is out. I'm surprised there aren't more animals in need of medical care."

"I did a little research while waiting for you. Statistics have shown relatively few animals are injured during wildfires. They usually escape the blaze, burrow beneath it or fly around it." Hannah backed against the wall. She folded her arms over her chest and shivered.

"Even the bigger game?"

"Apparently," she replied again, not taking her eyes off Andrew.

They stared at one another. Both of them leaning against separate walls, the space between them a chasm. He'd been an idiot to think sex wouldn't impact their working relationship. He couldn't stop thinking about her.

"The bid deadline is coming up. Is Bryan Plat still submitting?"

Andrew nodded. "Far as I know."

"And you're still backing Doctor Plat?"

"Yes, I still want Bryan Plat to win the bid. I also want it to be a fair contest."

Hannah toyed with the stethoscope hanging around her neck. "Why Bryan Plat? What's he got that makes him a more attractive candidate?"

Andrew rested his head back against the wall, looking up at the ceiling. He was stuck between a rock and a hard place. "He and I have been friends a long time. He hired me fresh out of vet tech college."

Straightening away from the wall, she blinked. "You used to work for him as a vet tech?"

"Yeah. He was the one who suggested I get into the animal control field."

"Does he need the business?"

He snorted loudly. "God, no. He's got a busy practice as it is."

"Do you really think he can fit the duties into his schedule?"

"Maybe, maybe not. If he wins the bid, he will do the job and do it well."

Hannah thrust her chin out. "Are you suggesting I can't do the job well?"

"Never said that." Holding his hands up in surrender, he kept his eyes steadily on hers. Her busy day revealed itself in her wrinkled surgical scrubs and tired expression. The last thing he wanted was to fight with her. If Bryan won the bid, would he see her again?

"No, but you meant it," Hannah's jaw tensed. "Don't forget, I have experience and training in shelter medicine. Current training. That's something your pal doesn't have."

"True, instead he has eight years of experience running his own practice. That counts."

Starting down the hallway back toward her office, Hannah fired back over her shoulder. "Perhaps. Have a nice day, Officer Kelly."

Andrew stared after her, regretting his position. With family on one side and a woman he was deeply attracted to on the other, his frustration was mounting. It was also likely he'd never get to see Hannah naked again.

***

"I love your apartment." Hannah said, setting down her purse.

Cortland pouted. "Thanks. I can't believe I've been here for four weeks already and you're just getting here to see it."

"Daddy came through?"

"I wouldn't be here if he hadn't. Actually, he was so happy to hear I had a job, he coughed up the money for the apartment *and* new furniture," Cortland chuckled as she led Hannah back into the stylish, white kitchen and started pulling down wineglasses.

Hannah snickered. "Did you tell him it was only part-time?"

"I did. And I told him it might turn full-time eventually. Frankly, he's thrilled to have me safely out of the house if you ask me." She reached into the refrigerator, pulling out a can of Diet Pepsi.

Cortland popped open the can and poured soda into the two glasses. "Salute!" The two women toasted each other.

"I do wish this were wine." Hannah eyed the fancy crystal wineglass, holding it up to the light. "Nice dark amber hue. No legs though."

Cortland chuckled. "No wine for either of us. There's a wildfire going on. We have to be fit for any emergency calls. I'm surprised we were able to sneak away for lunch." She kicked off her shoes before searching the cabinets. "God, remember our road trip escapes out to the Finger Lakes for wine tastings? I don't suppose there are any vineyards out here we can visit."

"Not that I know of. I haven't had a chance to look."

Having scrounging up some crackers and cheddar cheese, the two women sat down and dove into their impromptu lunch.

"So tell me again about Andrew Kelly. Why is he being such a dick about this bidding issue?" She picked up a cracker and slice of cheddar.

"From what Barbra Pari has told me, the guy he's backing is his brother-in-law. And he hired him out of tech school." Picking up a cracker, Hannah inspected it before popping it into her mouth.

"It's ridiculous." Cortland said between chewing on her snack.

"I know. After everything we've been through with Toby, I would have thought he'd have a little more respect for me now. But I guess family wins out." Hannah set down her glass, after only a sip.

Cortland scarfed down another cracker with cheese. "Maybe there's something else going on. Something he's not saying."

"That could be. It could very well be." Hannah's stomach knotted thinking of Andrew. *Why hadn't he told me about the family connection between him and Bryan Plat? But was it really any of my business? He made it clear who he preferred for the position. Did he need to say why?* Hannah scoffed. "I don't know why I let it get to me."

"Hmm," her friend mused, her eyes raised, and her head cocked. "Might it have something to do with your attraction to him?"

Staring into the bottom of her wineglass as if conjuring up wine instead of the soda, Hannah searched her soul. "I can't deny it. He's hot. And after the other night, well — let me just say he knows everything about pleasing a woman." She slugged back the last of the liquid, "which is why it can't happen again."

"WHAT?"

"It can't happen again. It was only sex. A comforting sexual escapade. And now it is over and never going to happen again. He and I have to work together, consequently, we can't indulge ever again. It was a mistake." Hannah paced the living room. "We were two consenting adults, but it was wrong. We never should have had sex. It's only opened a can of worms."

Cortland bounded off the couch and stopped her friend with a hand on each shoulder. Staring into her eyes she said, "It's a can of worms because you really like for him."

"The feeling, apparently, isn't mutual." Hannah's lip trembled as her eyes filled with tears. "I'll get over it. Him."

Scooping her friend in her arms, Cortland held her tight as she sobbed.

CHAPTER SIXTEEN

Rather than go back to the fire lines, Andrew returned to the shelter. It was time to check on the guests as he sometimes lovingly referred to them. He found nothing amiss during his walk through the cat room, nor in the kennel area. Some of the ten guests were a little subdued, while others paced back and forth in their kennels, their eyes darting about with worry. Andrew knew they could smell the smoke.

Walking back to his office bathroom to change his clothes, Andrew heard the police chatter on his two-way radio. Piney Ridge Road was closed to the north as were all the roads heading west off Route 17.

"Dispatch to ACO Kelly," a female voice called out over the radio.

Andrew jumped at the dispatcher's call. It was his normal means of communication with her, but he was feeling more than a little uneasy. He pulled the radio off his belt holster. "ACO Kelly to dispatch. Go ahead." His mind raced with the possible reasons for her call. Maybe there was another injured animal up on the fire line. Or maybe someone's dog was loose.

"Fire Chief Garness is reporting a wind shift to the southeast. Your shelter may be in danger. Chief is ordering evacuation of the premises."

"Roger that. Activating evacuation plans," Andrew responded.

Grabbing his keys, Andrew headed for the cat room. As swiftly as he could, he unlocked the closet door and removed four cat carriers. He transferred each unhappy cat into a carrier then hauled them out to the ACO van. On the second trip, he grabbed a handful of bungee cords from his office closet and secured the four cat carriers inside the vehicle using the cords.

Pausing a moment, he noticed a haze of gray smoke was descending over the entire area and building. He hoped the increased smell would not frighten the dogs further and make transferring them from the kennel to the van more difficult.

Next, he led each dog out of the building, one by one, placing each in one of the holding cages. Luckily, the vehicle was equipped with six cages. The dogs did not give him any problem but walked along with him as if they knew he was working hard to be their savior.

"Dispatch to ACO Kelly."

Andrew fumbled with the radio, "Kelly here."

"Chief wants to know if you're out of the area yet."

"Just getting into the van now. Heading out east on Route 34."

The radio was silent a few minutes as the dispatcher was conveying the information to the fire chief over the fire radio frequency.

"Chief says 'move it along', Kelly."

"Roger, moving out." Andrew jumped into the driver's seat, started it, and headed east on Route 34, away from the fire line.

Where was he going? The way to Bryan Plat's place was through the fire. It was going to have to be to Hannah's clinic. Perhaps she could put the ten animals up in her facility.

Andrew hit the contact number on his cell phone. The phone rang twice before being picked up.

"Colby County Veterinary Clinic. How may I help you?" Alissa's cheerful voice asked.

"Hi, this is Animal Control Officer Andrew Kelly. Can I speak with Doctor Woodbridge please? It's urgent."

"Hold on, please, Officer Kelly."

He pulled over to the side of the road to wait for Hannah to answer the phone. Fidgeting in his seat, tapping his fingers on the steering wheel. His eyes darted back and forth from the side mirror to the road behind him. The uneasiness in his stomach grew by the second as he waited for Hannah to pick up.

"Officer Kelly, what's up?"

"I've evacuated the shelter because the wildfire is encroaching on the property. I have a van full of animals. Four cats and six dogs. Is there any way your facility can hold them for a short time, at least until the fire danger is over?"

"It will be a tight squeeze here, but I think we can accommodate the animals. Are the cats in carriers, at least?"

He nodded, forgetting she couldn't see him. "Yes, the cats are in carriers. They can stay in them for a little while. With some help, the cages for the dogs can also be removed so they need not take up some of your care space. I need to get them out of the van. It's too hot to leave them inside the vehicle."

"Okay. Bring them over. We'll be expecting you."

Andrew put the cell phone down on the floor of the cab. He slammed his foot down on the gas pedal. The engine sputtered before a loud backfire sounded and the engine died. "Come on, baby, not now." Swearing through clenched teeth he turned the key in the ignition again. The engine did not start. He twisted the key again. The engine only moaned a little as if it wanted to turn over. Swearing thickly, he picked up the radio and called dispatch.

"ACO Kelly to Dispatch. I'm out on Route 34 near mile marker twenty-three. My vehicle is disabled. Can you send help?"

"Dispatch to Kelly. Roger that," she said.

Andrew kept trying the ignition while he waited for the dispatcher, swearing up a storm as the pit of his stomach clenched tighter and tighter.

"Dispatch to Kelly. Colby Garage Towing is on the way to your location. Also, update from Fire Chief Garness, the wildfire is less than a mile from your location."

Having kept his eyes off to the southwest, watching the billowing smoke rise from the horizon, Andrew already knew he was in trouble. "Tell the tow truck to step on it. I have a vehicle full of animals."

"Roger that, Kelly. Chief says jump in the truck and leave the animals if you have to."

BID TO LOVE

"Not going to happen, dispatch." Andrew said, his teeth clenched. He only hoped he was correct.

Waiting for the tow truck was like waiting for Christmas in July. No matter how hard he thought about it or wished it to be so, the truck was not going to get there any faster than it could. All the while, he kept one eye on the smoky horizon, now much closer to him, and one eye on the road looking for a tow truck. The gray haze of smoke became thicker and darker with a pinkish orange hue behind it as he waited. The smell was getting stronger and one of the dogs began to whine, causing several others to join in. Andrew's knee bounced impatiently as he wiped his forehead of sweat. After fifteen minutes, Andrew couldn't take the silence anymore. He picked up the radio and called dispatch again.

"Kelly to dispatch. Does the tow truck know of the situation? Looks like it's getting pretty close here."

"Roger."

Shit, he thought. Where the hell is it? He turned back to the encroaching fire line only to make out actual flames through the smoke. Off to the west, in the distance, he could hear a fire truck siren as if it were coming closer. In minutes, a bright red fire truck emerged on the scene, crossed to the shoulder of the highway and three firefighters jumped out. They went to the back of the rig, pulling out their hoses and dragged them straight out as far as they would go toward the fire line. On a signal from one of the firefighters, the hoses were pumped full of water and the two remaining firemen began hosing down the area in front of the fire with water.

His cell phone rang. "Kelly."

"Hey Andy," Bryan Plat said. "I need to talk to you about —"

"Can't talk now. I'm evacuating the shelter animals and my van broke down."

"Evacuating the shelter? What's going on?"

"Wildfires are heading for the shelter. I had to get them out of there."

Bryan guffawed. "Just leave them. They'll be all right on their own. And if not, well, there's no real loss, is there?"

Andrew's mouth dropped open, his mind unable to believe what he'd heard Bryan say. "I-I couldn't leave them. They're my responsibility."

"It's an emergency. Save yourself." Bryan advised.

Andrew stared at the phone in his hand a few seconds then he disconnected the call. His brother-in-law had suggested he leave his charges to fend for themselves, trapped in cages, during a wildfire? He rested his head on the steering wheel. This man, his former boss, the guy he had looked up to for so many years...was saying this?

His cell phone rang again. "Hello?"

"Where are you?" Hannah's voice called out.

Hannah. Hannah would never have told him to leave the animals. Never.

A honking horn drew Andrew's attention back to the east side of the highway. "Can't explain now. The tow truck is here."

"Tow truck! What —"

Andrew ended the call. The approaching tow truck drove past the van, made a U-turn, and then positioned itself in front of the broken-down vehicle. The tow truck driver got out and swiftly began work connecting the van to the tow truck.

"Get into the truck," he shouted out to Andrew. "I'm almost done here."

Andrew got into the passenger seat and closed the door. He said a little prayer that the animals wouldn't have too harrowing a ride on the hook of the tow truck. Given the option, he thought they would choose the uncomfortable ride to the real possibility of burning to death.

The driver got into the tow truck, put it in gear and they started down the highway. "We going to the garage?" the driver asked.

"No, to the Colby County Veterinary Clinic. I need to unload the animals there."

"Okay, on our way."

When the tow truck arrived in the parking lot of the clinic, a crowd of vet techs were standing by ready to unload the cages and carriers. In less than ten minutes all the animals were transferred into the facility and settled down. None seemed too shook up by the ride though one of the cats didn't stop howling until it was on level ground. Once the animals were out, the tow truck left with the van still attached, heading for the garage.

Andrew stayed behind with the animals to take care of them during their stay so the staff wouldn't have to, but the animals instantly became celebrities. Each was fed, given water, and either walked or given a litter tray. He was leaning against the wall in the cat area when Hannah showed up at his side.

"How did they all fair?" she asked.

"Well enough. Everyone is happy to be someplace stable. Thanks for taking us in. We'll be out of your hair as soon as we can get back to the shelter."

Hannah brushed a stray lock of hair away from her face and tucked it behind her ear. "Any news yet on the fate of the shelter?"

"I haven't checked yet," he said.

"What will you do if it's gone?"

Andrew shrugged one shoulder. "I guess I'll be calling the area towns to see if they can take one or two of the animals for us. And then I'll have to ask them to come get them if the van still isn't running by then."

Hannah put a hand on his arm and patted it. "Don't worry. I have faith everything will work out fine."

He warmed at her touch, and her words of faith. She understood how deeply his heart and soul cared for these creatures because she cared for them as deeply too. A lightness in his heart brought a smile to his face. "Thanks. Thanks for all your help and support." He put his own hand on top of hers, giving it a gentle squeeze.

"Dispatch to Officer Kelly," Andrew's radio squawked.

He pulled the radio out of its holster and held it up to his mouth. "Kelly, go ahead."

"Report of an abandoned dog in the fire zone. In the trailer park, on Route 6. Can you take the call?" Dispatch asked.

Hannah and Andrew stared into each other's wide eyes and said in unison. "Toby."

CHAPTER SEVENTEEN

Andrew swore under his breath. He turned back to Hannah. "You got a car I can borrow? I think she's sending me over the Myron Malin's for Toby. I wouldn't put it past the bastard to leave the dog behind."

"Let me get my keys for you," Hannah said, racing to her office for her car keys.

"Kelly to dispatch, I'll be in route as soon as I get some keys."

"Keep me posted Kelly, it's getting hot out there," the dispatcher said.

Hannah came trotting down the hallway, keys in hand. She dropped them into Andrew's open palm. "Here you go. Bring Toby here."

"I don't have much choice with the shelter under fire watch." Andrew ran for Hannah's Toyota, and jumped into the driver's seat. His foot slammed on the gas pedal, the little car fishtailing before peeling out of the parking lot in a cloud of dust.

Andrew raced to the outskirts of town. He passed a few cars going in the opposite direction, but the road before him was clear. In the distance ahead of him, the sky was full of billowing clouds of charcoal-colored smoke, growing larger and more ominous the closer he got to the cross road. His mind raced faster than the car, with thoughts of Toby being left behind to die, chained to that rusting hulk of a trailer. He wiped the sweat from his brow, his left foot pushing the gas pedal to the floor. This time Malin was going to lose the dog. One way or another. Andrew prayed it was by his rescue and seizure rather than the alternative.

He took a right turn onto Route 6 watching the landscape to his left. Not so far off, the hills were obscured with smoke from the fire. He kept trying to get a feeling for how fast the flames were moving as he drove.

If the route he had come in on was cut off, would he be able to continue on this road into the next county? How far did the fire extend? He wasn't sure, and he didn't want to take time to pull out his radio and start asking those questions. When he had the dog in the car, he'd worry about what way to go to skirt the fire line.

The trailer park came into view on his right side. Trying not to destroy Hannah's car, he quickly pulled off the road in front of Myron Malin's trailer. *Myron's truck isn't there.*

Leaving the engine running, Andrew hopped out of the car into a thick haze of gray smoke. He coughed, his eyes immediately starting to water. Rounding the front end of the car, he approached the trailer. There was no sign of life in or around it. Maybe he had it all wrong. Maybe dispatch was sending him to another animal at another trailer.

Andrew walked down the length of the trailer, coming to the back bumper. He saw the chain attached to the bumper and grabbed it. He hauled on the chain, feeling the resistance of weight at the other end. It had to be Toby. What kind of condition was he in? Physically as well as emotionally. Andrew got down on his hands and knees to look at the animal. Fearful, big brown eyes met his. "Come on, boy, let's get you out of here." Andrew pulled at the chain again.

Toby would not come. He seemed frozen to the spot. Andrew reached out and pet the dog's head. He did not growl or snap. He bowed his head and flinched, as if afraid to be hit. "It's all right pal, I'm not going to hurt you. I just want to get you out of here before it's too late, bud."

Feeling around the dog's neck, he grasped the collar and pulled as hard as he could. The dog's body slid toward him two feet. Andrew drew back and did it again. Once again, the dog's body slid toward him. Andrew did it one more time, this time the dog slid out from under the trailer, allowing Andrew access to his body. Still the dog would not get up. He lay quietly, his large brown eyes filled with terror, his entire body trembling.

After unhooking the chain from the dog's collar, Andrew picked up the dog, no easy feat even though Toby only weighed about fifty pounds. When he got to the car, he set the dog down, so he could open the car door. The dog, sensing the rescue, stood on his own four paws, still trembling, waiting for the car door to open. When Andrew had the door open, the dog immediately jumped inside, settling onto the back seat of Hannah's Corolla. Andrew shut the door, hustled around to the driver's side and got in. He pulled out his radio and called in.

"Kelly to dispatch," he said.

"Dispatch here, Kelly."

"Dispatch, I have retrieved the animal. What's my safest route out of here? Is Route 6 still clear heading back to town or should I cross into the next county?"

"One minute, Kelly." The dispatcher had probably gone to check with the fire department on the status of the surrounding area and the roads.

"Dispatch to Kelly, you're clear to return to town, but move it along."

"Roger that." Andrew said, starting the car. He wheeled the car into a U-turn, and floored the accelerator, taking the little car up to eighty miles per hour in less than a minute. As he flew down the roadway, Toby could be heard whimpering in the back seat. "Hang on there, pal. It's going to be a fast ride."

All the while Andrew drove, he thought this was it. This time, he would petition the court again for the seizure of this dog. Clearly his owner had abandoned him to the fire, leaving him to be burned to death, chained to the trailer. If that didn't say enough about Myron Malin, Andrew feared nothing but the death of the dog would satisfy the court.

Passage was a little dicey in areas. In a few places, the fire had overrun the roadway, leaving blackened char on the right side, while the flames slowly advanced toward town on the left. But in most places, the fire line was still off to Andrew's right, if not far, then at least far enough that he and Toby could safely pass.

They arrived unscathed at Colby County Veterinary Clinic. Sensing the danger was over, Toby was cooperative, getting out of the car and walking inside the clinic with Andrew hanging on to his collar.

Hannah stood, a hand pressed to her heart. She took one look at the two of them and sighed heavily. "Oh, thank God, I'm sure glad to see the two of you. I was getting worried."

"I'm sure glad we made it too. I don't think he needs a check-up but go ahead. I'm going to submit to the court again, based on this episode. Let me know if you find anything." Andrew said grimly. "Anything at all."

The fire stayed south of the shelter, leaving it untouched though smoky smelling. The mechanic found a clogged fuel filter which was easily replaced. After getting a ride to the garage in a police cruiser, Andrew drove the van back to the clinic, picked up the animals and returned everyone to the shelter by midnight.

He was on his way home when his phone rang. "Hello."

"Hello. See, everything worked out fine," Hannah said.

"Thanks for your help today. I don't know what I would have done without you."

"I'm glad I could help."

He pulled his truck into his driveway and shut it off. Nestled in the cab, the quiet of the early morning surrounding him, he sighed. "How's Toby?"

"Not too bad. He's definitely experiencing some effects of the smoke. But he should make a full recovery." Silence filled the phone line for a half a minute before Hannah added, "Well, I should probably let you get some sleep. You must be exhausted."

"Thanks, I am. I'll see you in the morning," Andrew said. He didn't know why he said that. *Wishful thinking?*

Her voice softened. "Good night."

"Good night." He was about to hang up when she called his name. "Andrew! I'm really glad you're all right."

She was gone before he could respond, but his heart felt lighter as the sweetness of her voice echoed in his ear.

CHAPTER EIGHTEEN

Cortland was off Labor Day weekend for a wedding and family reunion back home in Rochester, so Hannah was on coverage. Friday ended peacefully, but the moon was full. Things started going bad at sunrise.

Hannah's cell phone rang at six o'clock, summoning her to the clinic for an emergency patient. A German shepherd had been hit by a car after it escaped out the front door when the owner went out to get the morning paper. By some miracle, the dog sustained only a minor crack in his tibia leg bone that was easily set and cast within an hour.

Following the dog was a ferret showing signs of insulinoma, a tumor of the pancreas, and another dog with bloody diarrhea and hemorrhagic gastroenteritis, possibly due to round worm infestation. It was noon before Hannah had a moment to think.

When she sat down in her office to write notes on her morning patients, she noticed a manila envelope with a sticky note on it sitting in the center of her desk. The note read:

Hannah –

Enclosed is the information you will need to write up the bid for services for the Town of Colby

Animal Control Offices. Don't forget the bid is due nine o'clock Tuesday morning.

Barbra

Hannah sat back in her chair with a huff. She had totally forgotten she was supposed to work on the bid this weekend. Flipping over the manila envelope, she opened the flap and slid out the contents. It included a copy of the last bid for service Doctor Cambria had submitted, and a basic template for a new bid for service for this year's submission. Several more pieces of paper listed the requirements of the job which she began to scan.

The phone rang. Hannah picked up the receiver with one hand. "Hello." She continued to scan the requirements of the job and the application.

BID TO LOVE

"Doctor Woodbridge, there's another client on the way. Another dog hit by a car. I'll be putting him in room two."

Hannah recognized the voice of her veterinary tech, Alison Harrisan. "Okay, thanks," she said before hanging up. She set down the packet of papers. Reaching for her stethoscope, she draped it over her neck, took one last swig of cold coffee from the mug on the side of her desk and headed for examination room two.

Within thirteen minutes, the injured dog and its owner had arrived. The vet technicians on duty carried the dog into the examination room on the green canvas stretcher, followed by his owner, a young man. Hannah greeted the man, Mr. Saxon while the techs placed the stretcher on the stainless-steel examination table.

"Mr. Saxon, can you tell me what happened?"

The man placed one palm on his forehead. "Gosh, it happened so fast. We were out in the yard, playing catch with the kids. One of the kids missed the catch, and he ran after the ball across the street. He just took off on a tear, right into the path of an oncoming car. The kids are just a mess, as is my wife. And poor Blackie here." He gestured toward the black furred creature on the stretcher that still had not moved since being brought in to the room.

Hannah's heart raced as her palms went clammy. She stepped up to the table, pressing her stethoscope against the dog's chest, listening for breath sounds. Blackie. It was named Blackie and looked nearly identical to her Blackie. Except for a few tufts of white fur on the tip of his tail, the rest of the dog was completely black. His breath sounds were clear, his heart rate sounded elevated but strong. Both were good signs for now, though he was in shock. She ran her hands over every inch of Blackie's body, noting the injuries: possible fracture of the pelvis and back left leg.

"Did you pull the file, Alison?"

Alison gave a quick nod.

"What's the last weight?" Hannah asked.

"Sixty-five pounds," Alison reported.

"Okay, get me a port & Buprenex going. Lactated Ringers via IV."

"Mr. Saxon, from what I can tell, it looks as though Blackie may have a broken hind leg and possibly a broken pelvis. Normally, both are repairable with surgery. I won't know for sure until I have a look at x-rays. This could potentially be quite expensive. Would you like me to move forward with the x-rays?"

"My three kids adore this dog. Do whatever you have to do to save him," Mr. Saxon said.

Hannah turned to Alison, "Get him ready for pelvic and hind leg x-rays."

Three hours later, Hannah was out of surgery. Blackie had a badly broken leg, and a few broken ribs which had not punctured his lung. It was a relief to everyone his pelvis was not broken. The dog was in a medicated state in the intensive care area when Hannah stepped out to see Mr. Saxon. She found him in the waiting room with his wife, their children home with a sitter. "He's in rough shape. The next twenty-four hours will be tough, but he's fighting like a trooper. Do you have any questions?"

The Saxons left the clinic to go home for some rest while Hannah took up residence in the ICU, keeping a tight watch on Blackie. All the while, she was forced to relive the day she lost her own Blackie to a car sixteen years ago. Based on what she knew now, it was possible he could have been saved with modern veterinary care. But that care hadn't been available in her home town back then. They offered routine veterinary care and basic life-saving care. Fancy trauma treatments didn't come into vogue until well after her Blackie was long gone.

There were rural areas today that still did not treat veterinary trauma patients with the same gusto as human patients. Some people couldn't afford it. Some people didn't believe in putting their animals through it. Others were willing to pay for any treatment that might save the lives of what they considered their best friends, their family members, their surrogate children. And Hannah was not going to pass judgement on any of them either way. However, one of her first edicts was to not let money be an issue in treatment if some payment plan could be worked out.

Hannah camped out in the ICU so she could keep a close eye on Blackie throughout the night and into the next day.

Sunday morning Alison approached her. "Doctor Woodbridge, we have another patient. Possible foreign body ingestion."

Hannah sighed, palms on her knees. She gave them a slap before standing up. "Okay, lead the way." After x-ray confirmation of a hard, round object in the intestine, they prepped for surgery.

Thirty minutes later, Hannah pulled the scalpel across Higbee the Labrador's abdomen, leaving a tiny red line of blood to mark its path. Switching to sterile scissors, she enlarged the incision to a length of five inches. Below lay the red brown loops of the dog's intestines. Hannah pulled the intestines through the hole out onto the sterile towels covering the rest of the dog's abdomen. Slowly, she felt the length of the exposed intestine. The soft, slippery tissue glided through her hands, until she came to one area where a hard object filled the intestines, keeping it rigid. Hannah felt the hard object through the intestinal wall. It was about the same size as she had seen on the x-ray, making her sure she had the culprit.

Taking up her scalpel, she made an incision in the intestinal wall over the object, revealing a white rubber ball about one and one-half inches in diameter smeared with blood and brown goo. With gauze, she wiped the incision clean and widened it with her scalpel, just enough to pull the ball out of the intestines. With the object removed, she began to stitch up the hole in the intestinal wall.

Back aching, she stretched back her shoulders a few seconds, refocusing her eyes on the distant clock. It was one o'clock in the morning. She returned to her work, stitching up the numerous layers of abdominal walls and then the skin. When she was finished, Hannah stepped back from the operating table to give her technicians access to finish the job of cleaning the animal's wound area before moving him to the recovery.

Hannah pulled off her soiled gloves and the Tyvek gown protecting her scrub clothes. She glanced at the clock again. It was three in the morning. *I have to check on Blackie and get a few hours of sleep before tackling that bid application.* She rubbed her eyes and the back of her aching neck.

The door to the surgery unit opened and Alison poked her head in, her eyes full of remorse. "I'm sorry, doctor. You have another emergency case. Room one."

Hannah's shoulders slumped lower. She picked off the surgical bonnet and booties before heading for her newest patient. *So much for sleep. Doesn't anyone do that in this town on Labor Day weekend?*

A nudge roused her partially from her dream. A dream she didn't want to leave. She was driving a white corvette in a drag race, and she was winning, except the finish line kept moving farther away every time she got close to crossing it. The nudge was back, more insistent this time.

"Doctor Woodbridge. It's eight-thirty. Your patients are waiting."

My patients, Hannah thought. *Which ones? The ones I saw one after another like an animal conveyor belt? Or the normal scheduled patients on a Monday morning after a hellish weekend?* Then she remembered it was a long holiday weekend and yawned. If things kept going like this, she was going to have to get herself some back-up. Too many times, she had one patient waiting while she was seeing another. Not something she wanted to have happen with emergencies.

No, it's not Monday. It's Tuesday if it was a holiday weekend.

Hannah jumped straight up off the couch. "Oh my God, the bid!" *What time* – she checked her watch. It was twenty minutes to nine. She was going to miss the deadline for the bid submission. And she still had not written the damn thing yet. Hannah slumped back on the couch, hands over her face, eyes wet with tears she was too weary to cry.

"Doctor Woodbridge, call on line two." The intercom announced.

Hannah turned to her assistant, Alison, "You know, I think it's time I changed my name. Maybe I can get some peace if I do." She walked over to her desk and punched line two on the phone. "Hello, Doctor Woodbridge speaking."

"You didn't submit a bid." Andrew said.

"No, I had a hellish weekend of emergencies. I didn't have time to write it up, let alone time to bring it to the Chief of Police this morning."

"You've got ten minutes before I get there. Write it up. I'm on my way."

"How are you going to–"

"Leave it to me." Andrew said and hung up.

Hannah called out to Valerie, "Give me ten minutes. There's something important I need to take care of. Make my apologies to my next client. I'll be ten minutes late." She strode back to her desk and sat down.

She had looked at the previous bid several times over the weekend, so she had a general idea of the format. She turned on her computer and started typing. She had given the bid some scattered thought. All she had to do was get the figures down on paper. When a knock came at her office door, she was printing the bid.

"Come in," she called.

Andrew Kelly stepped in, dressed in his uniform. He shut the door behind him and leaned on it. "Finished?"

Hannah stuffed the bid into a manila envelope, sealed it and walked around her desk. "Ready. How are you going to get this submitted? It's after the bidding deadline."

"Simple. I tell them you gave me the envelope to deliver to the chief, and I forgot. Trust me, they won't penalize you for my mistake."

"But—"

"No buts. I'll handle it." Andrew said, grasping Hannah by the forearms and leaning over to kiss her on the forehead.

Her brain scrambled to keep up. "Why are you doing this?"

"I told you. I want this to be fair." He took the envelope out of her hand, opened the door, and left the building.

Hannah's intercom sounded. "Doctor Woodbridge."

She walked over to her desk and pressed the button. "Yes?" She recognized Valerie's voice.

"Doctor Woodbridge, Higbee has spiked a temp."

CHAPTER NINETEEN

She studied the chart for a third time. It didn't look good. She couldn't get her head around the fact the dog might actually be septic. How could it have happened? The entire foreign body removal procedure had gone without an incident of any kind. Everything was normal. The dog had been normal for two days. Now, suddenly, it was showing signs of a raging infection. And it could only be in his abdomen. It was the only logical possibility.

Maybe she had nicked his intestines and not noticed. He could be leaking digestive contents into his abdomen, causing the entire infectious process. She didn't believe she had. Wouldn't believe she had unless she saw evidence of it when she opened him up. That was the only thing she could do. Reopen the abdomen, inspect the intestinal incision for signs of leakage and the rest of the bowel for signs of perforation.

Hannah turned to the dog's assigned vet tech, Valerie. "Get him prepped for surgery. We'll have to go back and find out what's going on." Then she turned away and went to her office with Higbee's file still in her hand. After making herself as comfortable in her desk chair as she could, she read her surgery notes again. And again. There was nothing that gave her any ideas as to the cause of infection. The bowel had looked good. There hadn't been any signs of decay or strangulation and no signs of intestinal damage at all. It had to be something else.

The phone intercom rang. "Ready in room two with a patient. Also, Higbee's nearly ready in surgery."

"Super. Don't anesthetize him until I get there. I see this next patient and then head to surgery. Let my other patients know I'm running late due to an emergency. I'll see them as soon as I can."

The patient in room two was a quick check back after spaying. The incision looked to be healing and the ten-month-old cat, seemed to be doing fine. Hannah was in the surgery less than fifteen minutes later.

Entering the surgery room, she nodded to the vet tech to begin anesthetizing the dog. Higbee went under quickly and quietly. As she had done in the prep area, Hannah scrubbed the dog's incision site extra well, taking care to sterilize the surgical area. Then she began the arduous task of opening the abdomen again, in the same place, the entire time not knowing whether to pray she found the culprit or wishing she found nothing.

Once opened, the abdomen had the smell of foulness that comes from infection. Hannah winced as she carefully searched the abdomen but could not discern the origin of the infection. Ignoring the sweat already pooling at the base of her back and under her arm pits, she reached in and pulled the portion of affected bowel. She looked at the location where she had cut through the bowel wall to remove the rubber ball. The stitching looked intact. Even so, she still held her breath. There *had* to be something.

She bent over to get a closer look at her stitching. There was a little pinkness at the very corner of the incision. She squeezed the bowel at the incision site. Nothing came through the stitched tissues. She tried again, holding her breath. This time, a tiny bit of brown moisture showed up at the pinkened corner of the incision. The amount was so small it couldn't even be called a drop. But it was enough to wreak havoc in this poor dog's abdomen over the course of two days. "Damn it," she said. There it was. The last stitch hadn't been tight enough. Bowel liquids had been oozing out, infecting the dog. Hannah felt her heart sink into her gut. She had caused this poor creature to suffer the infection through her own fault.

Valerie held out the suturing needle. Hannah blinked back her tears, took it, and began to reinforce the stitches at the intestinal incision, taking extra care at the oozing corner. By the time she was satisfied, it almost looked like she had satin stitched the wound, a throwback to when she was a little girl, learning to embroider for a girl scout project.

Next, they flushed the dog's abdomen with twelve liters of warm sterile saline, trying to remove as much of the brown ooze as possible. Valerie suctioned the saline out carefully before Hannah began the long task of re-stitching the abdominal incisions closed.

Half an hour later, Hannah was backing out of the surgery room, to scrub down again. Higbee was off anesthesia and recovering well from the immediate effects of the surgery. His medication regime was modified to include high dose antibiotics to fight the current infection. Given that he was a healthy dog of a young age, he was expected to recover well. But Hannah wasn't feeling so sure yet. She had done him wrong once already, maybe he wouldn't respond well to the second surgery.

Hannah gave him one last look over before giving Higbee's owners a phone call to assure them he made it through the emergency surgery fine.

Later that day, when all the scheduled patients were gone, and Blackie's owners had been for a quick visit and left satisfied with his care, Hannah was still by Higbee's side, waiting for his temperature to go down as a sign that he was truly on the mend. That sign didn't come until nearly six o'clock the next morning. With a huge sigh of relief, Hannah handed over watch before setting off to go home for a shower, and a change of clothes.

When the dog woke again hours later, his tail began to wag, and he tried to get up but seemed to quickly realize the pain involved and lay back down. Back on watch, Hannah opened his compartment, stroking his head. Higbee licked her hand, perhaps just because it was there, perhaps in thanks. Hannah didn't care. It was a good sign. Tears burst from her as her heart lightened. A heavy weight was off her shoulders, at least temporarily. Higbee wasn't entirely out of danger yet. She settled down by the open kennel door, letting the dog rest his head contentedly on her thigh. They both fell asleep.

CHAPTER TWENTY

Children ran helter-skelter around her in their hurry to get to the rides at the Colby County Fair. Hannah took her time, taking in the games of chance on each side of the walk way, interspersed with booths hawking foods and drinks and things to buy. In her hand was a lemonade, complete with ice cubes and lemon slices. She stopped to scan her map of the fair. Somewhere here was the Animal Control Program's tent where Andrew Kelly had arranged a whole day of features such as Raptures Rescue and the Reptile SPCA. Also, in the animal control tent, in a quieter, controlled area, would be cages of animals available for adoption from this and surrounding towns. Hannah wanted to check on the welfare of the animals to make sure none were showing signs of being overstressed.

Halfway down the path, she found the tent. As she walked in, a program on feeding wild songbirds was underway. She looked around to find Andrew, but he was nowhere to be seen. *Perhaps he was in with the adoptions.*

Hannah walked over to the information desk to stand in line. Only ten people at a time were being allowed into the adoptions area. Asking for Officer Kelly, the volunteer at the desk confirmed her suspicion he was inside with the animals. Hannah introduced herself as the town's veterinarian and bypassed the lineup. She walked into the dimly lit area and saw sixteen cages, evenly split on either side of a plywood board. Those on the right held cats, while those on the left held dogs.

Standing before one of the cat cages was Andrew, talking with a middle-aged woman. He looked sexy as hell, all decked out in a crisply ironed dress ACO uniform. Hannah's blood stirred hotly in her veins, making her lady parts tingle with want. What she wouldn't give for another evening with him.

Their eyes caught. She saw his harden with hunger for a few seconds before softening. *He wants me as much as I want him.* A shiver ran down her spine.

He flagged her over.

"Ms. Barker, this is Doctor Woodbridge. She is the veterinarian who examined Freckles. Didn't you, Doctor Woodbridge?"

Hannah stopped beside the woman, looked into the cat cage, and recognized the occupant. "Yes, I did examine Freckles. She's a very calm and affectionate cat."

"And there's nothing wrong with her?" the woman asked.

"Nothing that I could tell. She will need three to four weeks to get adjusted to a new home, but I think she will be a splendid pet and make someone very happy."

The woman nodded to Andrew. "Where do I fill out the paperwork?" He showed her to a nearby table where adoption applications were available. Once the woman was seated, filling out the form, Andrew came back over to see Hannah. "Six possible adoptions today. This is great!"

Hannah's eyes scanned each cage. "Yes, but a few of them are showing signs of stress. Can they have a break? Maybe half an hour, shut off from visitors?"

"If you think it's really necessary. I can shut down the line out front for a little while. But I hate to miss such a great opportunity to get these guys adopted."

Contemplating the options, Hannah said, "They can't be at their best if they're stressed out. Look at that poor girl over there, the dachshund." Hannah pointed to a dachshund. "Just one look tells me she's petrified. Look, she's trembling. Any way you can take her out to someplace quieter, at the very least?"

Andrew thought a minute. "I can put her in the van and shut the doors with the air conditioning on. It's about the quietest place here."

"Yes, please do it. Getting her out of this heat will help too."

Walking over to the dachshund's cage, Andrew pulled a leash from his back pocket, opened the cage, and clasped the leash on the dog. Then he led the dog out the back of the tent.

While Andrew was gone, Hannah gave all the other animals a serious visual inspection. As she was doing so, a tall, dark haired, handsome man walked up to her. "Hello. Doctor Woodbridge, I presume. I'm Doctor Plat."

"Doctor Plat. It's nice to see you." Hannah said, hoping the fake enthusiasm in her voice would sound convincing.

"I see you two have met," Andrew said as he approached from the back of the tent. He looked over at Hannah. "You were right, she was relieved to get away."

Bryan Plat cocked his head at an angle and rubbed his chin. "Who are you talking about?"

"A dachshund named Samantha. Doctor Woodbridge noticed she was getting overly stressed, so I put her in the animal control van. She's much happier in there."

Bryan's eyebrow raised. "Is that what you were doing when I arrived? Assessing the animals' stress levels?"

"Yes. And I think Freckles is another contender, or will be very soon," she said, stepping aside so both men could see how the cat paced her small enclosure.

Andrew sighed. "I think she's got a new home anyway if the adopter checks out. Let me put her where it's quiet. Bryan, walk with me, will ya, while I carry the cage."

Hannah watched the two men head out of the rear of the tent, Andrew carrying Freckles' cage. Bryan certainly was handsome but that didn't mean he was the better qualified candidate for the job. Hannah suddenly hoped the Bid Selection Committee would see her good points: her education and experience. *Why didn't I submit a Curriculum Vitae with my bid?*

BID TO LOVE

***

Bryan walked ahead of Andrew, opening the tent flap and the van doors for him as he transported the cat carrier.

"So that's Doctor Woodbridge. Cute, but bossy, don't you think?"

Andrew turned back to him after securing Freckles' cage inside. "I wouldn't say bossy. Assertive and sure of herself, yes."

His brother-in-law folded his arms over his chest, frowned and looked Andrew over. "Um hm." Then his face broke into a wide grin. "You like her, don't you?"

"What? Me? Well, she's nice enough." He winced inside as he said the words. He turned his back to Bryan to hide a blush he could feel creeping up his face. Shutting the doors, he isolated the dachshund and cat together in the cool van.

"Hey pal — it's me you're talking to. Your brother-in-law."

"Yeah, and my former boss, both of whom want to win that bid." Andrew said quietly before turning back around.

"You don't have any influence on that decision, do you?" Bryan cocked his head.

Andrew shook his head vehemently. "None." *Thank God.*

"Too bad." Bryan patted him on the shoulder before wrapping his arm around Andrew's neck and giving it a squeeze. "I could really use a good word."

Andrew knew Bryan was trying to cash in on that tuition I.O.U. He hesitated and pulled away from Bryan's grip before heading back into the tent.

***

The two men returned, talking amongst themselves. As they neared, Bryan Plat stopped in front of her. "So, you have animal behavior experience, as well as shelter medicine experience?"

"Yes. I took an elective course in domestic animal behavior. It was very helpful. In all your years of practice experience I'm sure you are just as adept at recognizing the signs of stress as I am. You might not realize it."

He waved away her comment. "Oh, I'm familiar with the signs of stress in an animal. I'm a little surprised you would prefer the animals sit in the van rather than here where they would have a chance to be adopted."

The hairs on the back of Hannah's neck started to rise. "No animal, and no human for that matter, is at their best when they're under stress. You want a calm animal behavior to be projected when the animal is being viewed for adoption. Not some maniacal pacing or licking or drooling behavior. It turns off the potential adopter."

"Surely, the potential adopter realizes the animal is stressed and not at its best in a place like this. Besides, there are drugs that can help the animals relax."

"I don't give drugs lightly, and never for such a reason. If it's not a medical reason, it's not in the best interest of the animal."

The tall man loomed over her. "You gave some of the shelter animals Sileo for the Fourth of July fireworks."

Hannah's head snapped toward Andrew; her eyes boring into him. *How dare he discuss my methods with Bryan. He was all for the medication of those seven dogs at the time. Now I find out he was complaining about it?* "That was a different situation, and it was under consultation with Officer Kelly."

Hannah threw Andrew another icy stare. "I'm giving you my opinion as the town veterinarian. If you aren't liking the advice, you're free to do as you please."

Andrew spoke evenly but didn't appear happy. "Your advice has been sound. You do good work as the town vet."

"For now," said Bryan.

Hannah turned back to him, hands planted on her hips. "What do you mean, 'for now'?"

Bryan cocked his head jauntily. "Just that you're town vet, for now. Who knows what will happen at the bid selection on Monday?"

"One thing I'm sure of is you won't be selected." She turned on her heels and strode out of the tent, anger and fear tap dancing together in her belly. She needed to win that bid and she wanted to shove the win in Bryan Plat's smug face.

CHAPTER TWENTY-ONE

Hannah rushed into the room and abruptly halted. The meeting room at the Colby Town Hall was filled with metal folding chairs, only a few of which were occupied. Before the expanse of chairs, a panel of five sat at a folding banquet-sized table, looking out onto the small crowd gathered before them. Alone, unsure where to sit, she checked out who was where. Most of the audience members were seated in the front row. On the far side of the room stood Officer Andrew Kelly, in uniform. Andrew, glancing over his shoulder, saw her and gave her a wink and a tentative smile. Doctor Bryan Plat, seated in the center of the row must have seen Andrew's wink because he twisted around in his seat to see what was happening. Spying Hannah, Bryan's lip curled into a sneer before he dismissively faced forward.

If there weren't so many people here, I bet he would have given me the finger. Hannah chewed her bottom lip for a moment before squaring her shoulders. *He will not make me cower. I have as much right to be here as he does.*

She didn't recognize the two people sitting a few seats down from Bryan on his other side and assumed one was the third veterinarian competing for the bid.

Eyeing the room again, she spotted Dean Merryweather from the bank in the back of the room in the last row. Of course he would come to find out if she would procure the appointment. Hannah said yet another prayer that today would be the day she won the bid and her business loan. She gave Mr. Merryweather a courteous nod as he gave her a little wave and a smile.

Walking around the far side of the cluster of chairs, Hannah chose the third row on the end. Sitting down, she glanced at her hands as she bit her lip. *I wish Cortland had been free to come with me.* Cortland knew how important it was to get this appointment and had wanted to attend with Hannah for support. But somebody had to cover the midafternoon appointments so she could be here. Bracing herself by throwing her shoulders back and sitting tall in her chair, Hannah steadied herself to bear the bid opening alone.

Seeing she had taken a seat, Police Chief Dixon glanced at his watch, then cleared his throat loudly as he stood. "Thank you, everyone, for coming. This will only take a few minutes of your day," he said. "It's important to us that the Animal Control Program get not only the most cost-effective veterinary services, but also a talented and dedicated veterinarian who can respond to our calls at any time he or she is needed. Mayor Analis, would you like to say a few words?"

The woman on Chief Dixon's right nodded and rose as the chief sat down. "I am Mayor Anne Marie Analis. As the chief said, we are not looking so much for the cheapest bid but the best provider of services. Since this is the first time in twenty years that we've had more than two bidders, we, the bid selection team, have a real job to do. We hope you will bear with us as we open the bids. Then we will retire to my chambers to select the winner. If there is any question regarding a bid, we may ask for clarification here, now. That is why we asked the bidders to be present." She looked around the room at everyone in attendance. "Are there any questions?"

"None?" she raised an eyebrow before scanning the assembled body. "Great. Let's get started."

She sat down and picked up a manila envelope from the stack of three on the table in front of her. With a small letter opener, she sliced open the top of the envelope and removed the sheet of paper inside. "This is a bid from Doctor Paul Tabs, veterinarian in Chesterville. Total bid is $21,000." The mayor passed the bid packet to the man on her right who recorded the bid in the minutes of the meeting. A silent sigh escaped her lips as Hannah's posture in the chair eased. *That's one bid I have beat.*

As she reached for the second envelope, Hannah knew it was not hers, so her bid would be opened last. The mayor opened it with the same pen knife, extracting two sheets of paper. She looked at the first sheet, then lifted it to scan the second sheet. "This is a bid from Doctor Bryan Plat, veterinarian in Wilkesbury. The total bid is $20,500."

Her heart leapt at the amount. Her breathing sped up as she watched the mayor grab the last envelope, her bid. Opening it without fanfare, she removed one sheet of paper. She scanned the sheet then announced, "This is a bid from the veterinarian for Colby County Veterinary Clinic, Doctor Hannah Woodbridge. The total bid is $19,000." The materials were passed to the man on her right who recorded the information as he had the other two.

"If you folks would stay here please as the selection committee retires to my chambers for consideration of the bids, we will let you know our decision as soon as it is made." With that announcement, the entire team at the front table rose and walked out of the room.

The chatter began as soon as the panel left. Andrew stayed alone by the far wall. His friend, Bryan Plat and two other individuals, talked amongst themselves. Hannah sat alone, contemplating the bids. She was the obvious winner of the lowest bid but did that mean she was the actual winner? The other two veterinarians had thriving practices long before she had even finished with vet school. If they chose experience over lowest bid, she would be out of luck and up the proverbial creek when it came time to write her student loan repayment checks. She closed her eyes and lowered her head in a silent prayer that everything would turn out her way. It just had to.

"Doctor Woodbridge. Can you answer a question for the selection committee?"

Hannah's eyes flew open. The mayor stood in the doorway, a gentle smile on her face. The room had gone silent as all eyes turned to Hannah. Sweat sprouted on her brow and in her armpits. "Yes, of course." She faced Mayor Analis, trying to ignore the inquisitive stares around her. Her eyes shifted to Andrew, who looked as perplexed as she felt for being singled out.

"You didn't list the times you would be available or on call to animal control. Can you define when you intended to be available to meet their needs?"

Heat spread through her body as all eyes remained glued to her. "Anytime I'm needed. I'm willing to be called *anytime*, 24/7/365. Or provide coverage as required."

The mayor's mouth popped open at the announcement and the room went silent.

"You're sure?"

"Absolutely," Hannah said.

"Thank you for answering the question." The woman turned and left the room.

Slowly, conversation resumed, first at a whisper then rising to normal levels.

Hannah looked at the faces still glancing her way as they muttered. Her knees shook as she stood at her chair. *Walk it off.* She approached the nearest window at the back of the room. Squinting against the afternoon sun, she stared unseeingly at a couple of baseball fields beyond the town hall parking lot. Quietly, she hummed the hymn Amazing Grace to keep from overhearing the chatter.

The conversation stopped behind her and she heard feet shuffling into the room. She turned to see the selection committee returning. Hannah quickly resumed her seat, her knees still trembling.

Once the committee members had all resumed their seats at the head table, the mayor said, "We have made a decision. First, we thank each of our bidders for participating in this year's bidding process." Mayor Analis picked up a sheet of paper and read from it, "The bid we chose is from Doctor Bryan Plat."

Shocked, Hannah sat still in her seat, afraid to move. A wave of nausea rolled through her gut. If she moved, she would throw up right there in her lap and on the floor. Swallowing hard to keep the bile down, she watched as Bryan Plat rose and headed her way. Andrew started to follow him from the far side of the room. She held her breath as he approached. *Is he going to shake my hand?* Bryan stopped in front of her and looked down at her in her seat. His lip curled into a sneer. "So how does it feel to lose, bitch? Better luck next time, if you dare."

Hannah flinched backward as though she'd been slapped across the face. She jolted up, her chair falling over backward and her purse dropping from her lap to the floor. She opened her mouth for a rebuttal, but no sound came out.

"What's the matter? Cat got your tongue? You're pathetic," Bryan spat before turning his back to her and stalking out of the room.

Tears blurring her vision, Hannah watched Andrew's approach, his face scarlet and fists bunched at his side. Eyes narrowed, he spoke through thinned lips, "Don't pay any attention to him, Hannah." When he reached out to grasp her hand, Hannah recoiled.

"Don't touch me." Hannah stepped backward. She picked up her purse and hurried for the door. She paused as she passed Dean Merryweather, who had waited for her.

"I'm sorry," he said, his eyes pained with remorse.

With a toss of her head, Hannah whispered, "I understand," then she bolted for the doorway.

Sprinting down the hall, she found the ladies restroom, barging through the stall door just in time to empty her stomach.

***

Blood pressure rising and gut clenching, Andrew stood in the hallway watching Hannah scurry to the ladies' bathroom. He glanced in the opposite direction trying to see over the heads of the committee members who now filled the corridor. At the far end of the hall the exterior door opened, and the back of Bryan's head disappeared as he passed through. Jaw hardening, Andrew ran down the passageway as best he could. A shove at the door had it slamming against the outside wall. The lone figure of his brother-in-law climbed into his car, silhouetted against the sun.

Afraid he'd get away, Andrew kicked into a power sprint. He flung himself at the car, wrestling away the door as Bryan tried to shut it.

"Hey —" Bryan called out. "Let go."

Andrew glared at him, his teeth ready to break they were locked so tight.

"What?" Bryan gestured with his hand. "Aren't you going to congratulate me?"

His body rigid, his hands fisted, Andrew's eyes bore into him. "Are you kidding me? After what you just did to Hannah you expect me to congratulate you?"

"She's just a cun—"

Andrew hauled Bryan out of his car and laid him out of the asphalt parking lot. He stood over his shocked brother-in-law, panting from the exertion, his right fist throbbing, two knuckles bleeding.

Bryan lay on the pavement a few second, his face registering fear and surprise before sitting up. He tossed his head back and hugged his hand to his jaw. "Son of a bitch! What'd you do that for?"

A minivan pulled into the space beside them.

"Don't you ever refer to Doctor Woodbridge in that manner. Never." Andrew seethed through clenched teeth. Reaching down, he grabbed Bryan by his shirt lapels and dragged him to his feet. "You owe her an apology. Now."

"Like hell—"

"What's going on here?" A female voice broke in and a pregnant body tried to step between the two men. Kimberly Plat looked from one to the other, her face pinched, expression hard. "You're scaring Daniel."

"Nothing. Nothing's going on." Bryan jerked himself out of Andrew's grasp and rubbed the left side of his jaw, testing its motion.

"Your husband just verbally attacked Doctor Hannah Woodbridge after he won the bid."

Andrew stepped backward. He might not believe in the power of love between these two, but he believed if anyone could get Bryan to apologize to Hannah, it would be Kimberly.

Kim's eyes widened in disbelief. "What did you say?"

"It doesn't matter." Bryan dusted off his clothes refusing to meet her eyes.

Turning to Andrew, she asked him. "What did he say? Please tell me the truth."

Andrew glared at Bryan over Kim's head.

"Andrew, tell me." Kimberly demanded, her hands on what she could find of her hips, fury lacing her words.

"He said, 'How does it feel to lose bitch?' And just now he called her the c-word." Andrew's face still tense, he added, "And I decked him for it."

Kimberly's face whitened with rage. Getting right in her husband's face, she spoke softly but firmly. "You — you are going to apologize to that woman."

Bryan stared back at her. "Like hell I will."

Pointing her finger at his nose, she declared, "So help me God, you can find another place to live until you do." She turned and waddled back to her minivan where Daniel waited in the back seat. The boy waved at his father and godfather. Both men waved back solemnly as the vehicle drove away.

"Thanks, asswipe." Bryan muttered. "Men are supposed to stick together." Ignoring him, Andrew stepped aside as Bryan got back into his car. "I don't suppose you'd put me up for the night."

"I won't even consider it until you've apologized." Andrew crossed his arms over his chest.

"Thanks for nothing." The car engine roared to life, the door slammed shut and he peeled out of the lot.

Andrew leaned over, his hands on his knees, trying to calm down. *Did Hannah leave already?* He looked to where her Toyota had been parked at the other end of the lot. The space was empty. He briefly wondered if she had seen their altercation. She might not have been aware of it all the way across the lot.

He picked his cell phone out of his pocket and hit her number.

CHAPTER TWENTY-TWO

Hannah sat in her car with a white-knuckled grip on the steering wheel, a roaring in her head repeating the name Bryan Plat. *How could this have happened? That rat-fink Andrew had to be behind this. Him and his pal Bryan.* Unsure how she got home, she had no recollection of what route she took to get there and how much traffic she encountered. *How could I have been so stupid as to trust him? What an idiot I've been to trust him. All I gained is a slap in the face. I can't believe what that jerk said to me?* Fresh tears sprouted, following the course of the previous drops down her face.

She trudged to her apartment, opening the door to a tail-wagging Maggie Mae. Her heart thawed slightly as the dog nuzzled her hand. Maybe nobody else wanted her around, but Maggie Mae did. Hannah sank onto her knees and pulled the dog into a tight hug. Burying her nose in the soft brown curls of the dog's fur she inhaled the doggy goodness. Maggie squirmed away, escaping the confines of Hannah's arms.

"Not you too," Hannah cried, before remembering Maggie disliked being held.

Maggie nuzzled her mama's hand again, and Hannah responded, patting the dog along her back. "Thanks, baby girl. I need some extra love tonight."

The cell phone rang, forcing Hannah to reach into her purse for the phone. She pulled it out, frowned at the screen name and hit talk. "Hello."

"Hannah, I'm sorry," Andrew said.

She sat up straight, dropping her purse on the floor, scattering the contents across the oak wood. A scared Maggie scampered away at the noise. "Really. You're sorry? Why are you calling, Andrew, because it's certainly not to tell the truth?"

"No, Hannah, please listen. I really am sorry. I know you seriously wanted the appointment. And I'm sorry for what Bryan said. It was uncalled for."

"You know what, Andrew, I've had enough of you for one evening." Hannah clicked off the call.

Thirty seconds later, the cell phone rang again. The screen revealed it was Andrew again.

Hannah hit the ignore button and the ringing stopped. She contemplated shutting off the phone but since she was on call at the clinic, she couldn't.

She lay flat on her back on the floor and stared at the light fixture on the ceiling. Maggie came over and laid beside her. Hannah reached out to the dog for comfort. "What are we going to do, Maggie? We can't pay the student loans."

Maggie huffed then lay her head on Hannah's abdomen.

Banging on the door woke her up. Startled, she bolted upright, not knowing what time it was or how long she had been asleep. Heavy pounding on her door echoed through the apartment. Maggie Mae sprang to her feet and began to bark wildly.

"Wait a minute," she called out. "Maggie, enough." The dog looked at her strangely, before ceasing her barking.

Hannah got to her feet. They both went to the door. Hannah opened the door two inches, peering out. Maggie poked her brown nose out the crack and sniffed.

Andrew waited on the other side, his face dark and pinched.

"What do you want?" Hannah held the door closed to a crack.

Andrew ran a hand through his hair, messing it up further. "I want to talk with you about earlier tonight."

Hannah breathed heavily. "Look, I don't want to talk about it, okay. What's done is done. I lost the bid. It's over. Besides, enough has been said." She closed the door in Andrew's face, but he grabbed it at the last second and pushed it back open enough to poke his head through cautiously.

"Look, there's something I think you should take a look at before you give up the fight."

The dog's nose inched at the opening to sniff Andrew on the other side of the door. Maggie whined her displeasure at not being able to get closer to him. Hannah braced her weight against the door, still determined to shut it. "What could possibly make a difference?"

"Let me in and I'll show you."

Hannah hesitated, but Maggie Mae had other plans. She wanted to see her second favorite person in the whole world, so she kept wedging her nose between the door and the jamb until Hannah, afraid to hurt the dog, let it go. Maggie scurried out into the hallway, running circles around Andrew's feet, barking and yipping with glee. Stepping aside, Hannah let the man into her home for the second time in her life. Briefly, she wondered if he remembered anything about being there only a few weeks ago. The memory of him carrying her, half naked, to her bedroom and the things they did there still set her insides aquiver.

Andrew shuffled inside the foyer, trying not to step on or trip over Maggie who twisted herself around his ankles like a cat. Fisted in his left hand were sheets of paper which he waved at Hannah. "You have to read these."

"What are they?"

"They're the bidding rules for the Town of Colby Animal Control Program."

"Why?"

Andrew rolled his eyes. "Just read them." He thrust the papers at her again, but she refused to take them.

She crossed her arms over her chest. "I've already read them, Andrew. Before I submitted the bid."

Andrew walked over to her dining table and began to spread the papers out on the table, before sitting down on the edge of a chair.

BID TO LOVE

Glowering at him, Hannah watched.

He sat back in his chair, having arranged the papers to his satisfaction, and gestured toward the empty chair across from him. When she made no move to sit, Andrew kicked back the chair under the table with his foot. "Sit down and read it again."

Eyes flashing venom, she grabbed the chair by the rail, pulled it out, sat and folded her hands in front of her on the tabletop. "Why?"

Andrew sighed as he picked up the first paper on his left. "This paper begins the description of the services the bid winner will provide to the Town of Colby. More specifically, it explains all the duties of the job."

Hannah took it and began to read silently. Andrew sat quietly but fidgeted as her eyes scanned the pages. He stabbed at the paper. "Read it aloud."

She glared at him, "I'm not going to read the whole thing aloud."

Rolling his eyes, he flopped back in the chair. "So just read me the salient facts."

Hannah frowned. "The wording is a little odd. It says, '...said veterinarian will remain in the Town of Colby while not actively participating in the duties of the job and shall participate in the making of regulations pertaining to the welfare of animals, domestic and wild, within the borders of the Town of Colby.' "

"Good, you got to the right spot." Andrew said before snatching the paper out of her hand.

"Hey —" she blustered.

"Now read this." Andrew slid forward another sheet of paper.

Again, Hannah skimmed the page. "It describes in more detail the responsibilities of the job holder."

"Such as..." Andrew prompted, spinning his hand as if winding a ball of yarn.

"'The veterinarian shall be accessible within Colby at all times, unless covered by another qualified person during times of vacation, illness or holiday.'"

Hannah rubbed her eyes. *What is he getting at?* She didn't have a clue and she was tired and quickly becoming ornery. "Get to the point, Andrew."

"Thirdly," he said as he picked up the next sheet of paper. "Now this is important, so read carefully. This is from the Town of Colby statutes. I highlighted the important phrase."

After taking the page, Hannah read aloud. "'Only those persons who are citizens of the Town of Colby and are duly elected or appointed by citizens of the town or the mayor may participate in the formation of regulations pertaining to the Town of Colby.'"

Hannah set the paper down.

"Ohmygod," Hannah sat up straighter, her eyes wide and bright. "So, Bryan Plat can't be veterinarian for Colby. He's in the town of Wilkesbury, in Colby County. He may be just over the line but he's still not a member of Colby and he can't be in town while he's working at his practice. Neither can Paul Tabs. He lives and works in Chesterville, in Danville County. Both men are ineligible for the job based on the description and requirements of the job and the requirements of a person making regulations for the Town of Colby."

She stopped talking to let the information sink in. Her jaw hung open, her hand over her gaping mouth.

Leaning toward him across the table, Hannah said, "So, neither individual is truly eligible for the job. Their bids should have been disqualified." She got up from the table and paced to the living room and back again.

Andrew sat back in his chair and smiled as he watched her.

"I have to appeal the selection. I will set up a meeting with the mayor, describe the situation, read her what I just read if necessary.

Make her see it was all wrong. I'm the only qualified candidate. I should have won the bid."

Hannah hesitated before him, "Do you think she'll listen?"

"She has no choice. She'll listen to any plausible explanation you have to invalidate the current selection, so long as it can hold the proverbial water."

"Why do you think the committee didn't realize the issue?"

Andrew shrugged his shoulders. "Who knows? Maybe because it has always been Doc Cambria and he always met the qualifications."

Silence engulfed the room as Hannah began pacing again. Once more she stopped in front of Andrew. "So, why are you bringing this to my attention. You got what you wanted. Bryan got the job."

Andrew looked down at his hands. "Maybe I changed my mind."

Hannah stared at him in disbelief. It didn't seem plausible that one day he'd be rooting for his brother-in-law, and the next, he'd be helping her win the bidding process. "What's the real reason?"

Andrew shrugged. "Bryan was such an arrogant dick about winning the bid I couldn't stand it. And the way he attacked you was completely uncalled for. You didn't deserve it."

"So, now you want me to get the bid?" Hannah asked.

Andrew met her gaze directly. "Yes, I want *you* to get it."

Hannah had the urge to throw her arms around Andrew and give him a huge hug, but she was still angry at him for not having backed her from the beginning. And he had yet to mention Bryan was his brother-in-law. However, he *had* shown her how to get the selection rescinded. She owed him a concession. She held out her right hand for a shake.

Smiling broadly, Andrew took her hand as if to shake it but then drew her close against him. Hannah inhaled sharply as her body was crushed against his chest, her heart thundering. As he tipped his head down to kiss her, his cell phone rang. With a groan, he let her go and pulled the phone out of his pocket.

"Kelly." His free hand dug in his pants pocket for his notepad and pen. "Now? Okay, I'm on my way." He ended the call. He shoved the pad and pen back into his pocket without writing anything down. "Got to leave. My sister's in labor and I have to watch her son." His eyes downcast, he sighed and slumped his shoulders.

"That's okay. I think I've had enough excitement for one day."

She walked him to the door. Drifting over to the window, she waved as he drove out of the driveway. She noted he hadn't acknowledged that Bryan and his sister were married. And that his nephew was Bryan's child as well. She tossed this difficulty aside. He had come to her to help her with the bid selection. With the information he had provided, she could fight the selection and win. Her mind racing, the weight on her shoulders eased a little while her heart galloped with the possibility that all was not yet lost.

CHAPTER TWENTY-THREE

Getting an appointment with the mayor was much easier than Hannah expected. Kind and accommodating, Hannah did get the impression the woman was sincerely interested in listening, just as Andrew had said.

She showed up for the meeting at eight o'clock in the morning, the best time the two women could find to meet between their busy schedules. Hannah wore her usual working attire of casual trousers with neatly ironed white oxford shirt. For a little bling, she added a simple string of turquoise beads she had picked up during a trip to Arizona as a teenager with a matching bracelet and a sterling silver ring and earring set that always brought her luck. She had worn them during her board exams and had passed with a high score. Satisfied with her appearance, she felt confident she could argue her way into the position easily.

Seated in a chair outside the mayor's office, Hannah felt as if she were waiting to see the principal at school. Only this time there was so much more at stake than a silly demerit or detention. She had to win the bid back. There was no other way for her to pay back her student loan debts and her business debts at the same time. The fall in clientele at the clinic was being felt. Income had dropped noticeably. She was hoping she didn't have to lay off any of the staff. For now, they were busy enough and profitable enough to keep in the black. As Barbra Pari had said, the winter months might be significantly leaner. Getting this bid might not help at the clinic, but it would keep her from defaulting on her student loans. She didn't know what the authorities would do to her if she defaulted. Visions of jail time raced through her mind as she thought of it, stirring up her anger.

Settle down, I won't let that happen without a bare-knuckles fight.

The door opened beside her, and Mayor Analis stepped out into the hallway. "Doctor Woodbridge, please come in. I'm sorry to keep you waiting."

"Thank you." Hannah said as she followed the mayor through the receptionist's area and into her private office. She held on to her purse tightly, trying not to let the trembling of her hands show.

"Please, have a seat," the mayor said, gesturing toward an empty chair in front of the desk.

Hannah settled herself on the edge of the seat, her back ramrod straight.

Mayor Analis eyed her with curiosity. "What can I do for you, doctor?"

"Mayor, I'd like to appeal the bid results on the basis that two of the three applicants for the position should have been disqualified from the process." Hannah opened her purse and removed the sheets of paper that Andrew Kelly had given her.

The mayor inspected her with a sharp twinkle in her eyes. "By what reasoning?"

Unfolding the sheets, Hannah pointed to the one on top and said, "Well, it says here in the description of the duties that the winning bidder *must* be within the borders of the town of Colby while on duty unless there is coverage."

The mayor took the sheet of paper with the passage particular to Hannah's argument highlighted. She picked up her reading glasses and began to read.

"Is there anything else?" the mayor asked, gesturing toward the remaining papers in Hannah's hand.

"Yes. It also stipulates that the bid winner will participate in the formation of regulations for the protection of animals, domestic and wild, in the Town of Colby. And yet, the town's statutes require that any person participating in the formation of regulations for the Town of Colby must be a citizen of Colby *and* must be either elected by the citizens or appointed by the mayor."

Mayor Analis took the remaining two papers Hannah held out with the passages highlighted as well. She looked them over and frowned.

Hannah swallowed before continuing. "Neither Paul Tabs nor Bryan Plat are citizens of Colby. Neither of the men work in the town. They cannot be in town during their coverage, yet still be performing the duties of their own businesses in their own towns. Nor can they, by virtue of their lack of citizenship in Colby, participate in the formation of regulations," Hannah said. "I am asking that the selection committee reconsider the bids based on these facts, rescind Bryan Plat's appointment, and disqualify both Bryan Plat and Paul Tabs' bids. As the only person who can meet all the requirements, I alone should be the winner of the bid."

Setting aside the papers on her desk, Mayor Analis stood. She smiled warmly and said, "I will reconvene the selection committee to discuss the matter. That is all I can promise at this time."

"Thank you. I appreciate your time and consideration of this matter," Hannah rose and held out her right hand.

Mayor Analis shook it. "Good luck to you."

Hannah exited the mayor's chamber, walked through the receptionist's area and out into the hallway. She made it all the way to her car before the tension of the moment hit her full force. Tears poured down her cheeks so fast and furious, she had to use her shirt cuffs as wipes. It was several minutes before she was able to gather herself together again. When she did, she reflected that the mayor had not offered any hope that the bid would be disqualified. Nor had she said what time frame would be involved. Hannah was going to have to wait to see what the outcome was in whatever time it was going to take.

CHAPTER TWENTY-FOUR

The court case seeking to rescind custody of Myron Malin's dog, Toby was set for September fifteenth. Andrew arrived at the courthouse a full hour ahead of schedule to be sure he was on time. Dispatch had been notified to hold all his calls or, in the case of an emergency, to call for backup from Chesterville. There was no way he was going to miss presenting his testimony.

As expected, Myron Malin had brought along a lawyer, confident in his ability to keep his dog. His lawyer felt there were no grounds on which to base the complaint Malin had neglected and left his only dog to perish. And that is how the lawyer pleaded the case before Judge Shapiro in his opening statement.

"Mr. Malin is not a bad man, or a hurtful man. He simply forgot about his dog. He was in town when news of the wildfire spreading out to his trailer park became known. He didn't consider it safe to go back to the trailer to get anything, not even his dog. Would the roads have been clear enough at that point to even allow him access to his trailer park? Would the dog come willingly from the premises given the frightening situation transpiring at the trailer?"

The lawyer went on to argue that this was the third time Town of Colby Animal Control Officer, Andrew Kelly was trying to remove the dog from Myron Malin's possession. That it was something with Mr. Kelly, not Mr. Malin, that kept him coming back to the court time and again to try to seize ownership of the dog. One would be tempted to call such an issue harassment. One would also call him a stalker for his daily visits to the Malin premises to check on the dog's welfare. It was clear that Mr. Kelly, not Mr. Malin was the party that needed court intervention.

Andrew gritted his teeth at the insinuation that he was stalking Myron Malin. Fortunately, the prosecutor of the case for the Town of Colby fought back, explaining that the welfare of every animal within the town boundaries was Mr. Kelly's job and concern. He had every right to be checking on the safety and health of the dog, as part of his employment. Regarding leaving the dog behind, it was inconceivable that someone would leave behind a loving pet. And it would be shown that Mr. Malin had no consideration for his dog whatsoever. Based on these grounds, the animal should be surrendered to the Town of Colby.

Judge Shapiro listened intently, knowing the history of Myron Malin and knowing how many times Andrew Kelly had tried to seize the dog from him.

First to take the stand was Andrew, who related the events on the day he rescued Toby from the trailer as the wildfire set in.

"I pulled up to the trailer and could hardly even see its back bumper, the smoke was getting so thick in the area."

"What did you do then, Officer Kelly?" the prosecuting attorney asked.

"I got out of the vehicle and walked over to the area where I knew that dog was chained."

"Did you find the dog and if so, what condition was he in?"

"I found the dog, still chained to the trailer's bumper. He had crawled far under the chassis of the trailer." Andrew watched the attorney as he paced the floor in front of the witness stand.

"What did you do next?"

"I tried to get Toby to come to me, but he wouldn't. He seemed too afraid to move, with all the smoke in area — it must have scared him. So, I had to grab hold of his collar and drag him out from under the trailer."

"Was he cooperative once he was out from under the trailer?"

"I sensed he was. I put my leash on him and released him from the chain holding him to the trailer. He got up and I was able to lead him to the vehicle waiting in the driveway."

"Did the dog continue to cooperate or did he fight you?"

Andrew smiled, "No sir, he was very cooperative. He seemed to know I was leading him out of the danger area, and he got into the vehicle without any trouble."

"What did you do then, Officer Kelly?"

"I also got into the vehicle, and we headed out of the wildfire. I did check in with the police dispatcher to find out if the routes back to town were still clear. She conferred with the fire department to find out if they were open. We returned to town without incident."

"Where did you take the dog, Officer Kelly?"

"I brought the dog to Colby County Veterinary Clinic. Doctor Hannah Woodbridge was there, waiting to examine the dog for an evaluation."

"What did she find?"

"She found the dog to be underweight and skittish. He had also suffered adverse effects from the smoke in the air," Andrew said, his eyes fastened on Hannah.

"Did the dog remain at the clinic?"

"Yes, Toby was kept at the animal clinic to assure us that he was recovering from any additional symptoms of smoke inhalation. Three days later, I was able to pick him up and bring him to the animal control shelter."

The attorney stopped pacing, pausing before the judge's bench. "When did Myron Malin come to the shelter to remove Toby?"

Andrew's eyebrows rose. "Mr. Malin didn't show up to take Toby until seven days later."

"Did he give any reason as to why he was so late to pick up his pet?"

"He only said it was the earliest convenience he had to pick Toby up. Seven days after the wildfire."

"Was the dog happy to see him?"

Shaking his head, Andrew said, "No sir, he was trembling when Myron Malin showed up at his kennel. He shrunk back to the farthest part of the kennel, far away from the door where Mr. Malin was standing, calling him."

The attorney stared at Mr. Malin. "Did the dog show any signs of wanting to go home with his owner?"

Andrew too, glanced over at Myron Malin, seated at the defense table. "No signs at all. In fact, every sign he gave suggested he didn't want to leave the kennel with Mr. Malin."

"Tell us your history with Mr. Malin."

"Mr. Malin does not have a good history with animals. In the past, he has had to surrender his previous dogs to authorities, the case number was 92-347 in this court system."

"Was the surrender his own doing or were the previous dogs actually seized by the courts?"

"The previous dogs were seized by the court."

"Do you have any witnesses to the event that took place during the wildfire?"

Again, Andrew shook his head. "No, there were no witnesses to my taking the dog from the trailer. I do have lots of witnesses to the fact he was taken to the Colby County Veterinary Clinic. Including Doctor Hannah Woodbridge who examined the dog."

"Is Doctor Woodbridge here in this room?"

"Yes, she is sitting over by the prosecution table."

"Thank you, Officer Kelly."

Next, the defense attorney interrogated Andrew. He walked over to the witness stand and stopped directly in front of Andrew.

"Officer Kelly, how long have you been with the Town of Colby as their animal control officer?"

"I've been with them for five years."

"You said you had no witnesses to the events that took place at the trailer park, is that right?"

"Yes, I was the only one there that I could see. No one else around."

"So, everything you said about Toby cowering under the trailer and having to drag him out from under it, that's all *your* testimony and we have no one to corroborate it."

Andrew shrugged. "Yes, that's probably a true statement."

"No further questions, your honor," said the defense attorney before returning to his seat beside Myron Malin.

***

Next up on the stand was Hannah. She was sworn in and sat on the chair beside the judge's seat to give testimony.

"Doctor Woodbridge, thank you for coming today. Would you please tell the court your credentials?"

"Thank you for asking. I received my bachelor's degree in animal science Connecticut University and my Doctor of Veterinary Medicine degree at Cornell University. After my graduation, I interned with PAWS Chicago, doing work in their ASPCA clinic there and also in their shelter."

"Thank you, Doctor Woodbridge. Did you, in fact, perform an examination on the dog in question, Toby, owned by Mr. Malin."

Hannah folded her hands in her lap. "Yes, I did. He was brought to my clinic by Officer Andrew Kelly, after having been rescued from the wildfire on the outskirts of town."

The prosecuting attorney paced in front of the witness stand, "What day was this, doctor?"

Hannah looked over at Andrew. "It was August twenty-sixth of this year."

"Can you please tell us of your findings at the examination of Toby?" he said, stopping beside the stand and remaining still.

"Sure. Toby, at the time, was about fifty-six pounds, which is about ten to twenty pounds less than I would expect considering the type of dog he is."

"What type of dog is Toby?"

Hannah smiled. "He's a lab and pit bull mix."

"So, the dog was underweight?" The attorney turned to face Mr. Malin as he waited for Hannah's answer.

"Yes, he was underweight, and I had no way of knowing if he was vaccinated for anything. We didn't know where Mr. Malin has been taking Toby for veterinary services such as rabies vaccines and the like."

"What was your initial impression of the dog?"

Remembering the dog's condition, Hannah frowned. "He was underfed and under exercised. His leg muscles were not very strong, flaccid almost. He had pressure sores on his haunches and pressure calluses on his elbows."

"What does that indicate to you, in your professional opinion, doctor?"

Clasping her hands together, she boldly stated, "That indicates to me that the dog is spending way too much time lying down and not nearly enough time being walked." Fearing her anger would be reflected in her expression, Hannah avoided looking at Malin.

"Did you find anything else?"

"On closer examination, he was found to have some signs and symptoms related to smoke inhalation. His coat had a smoky odor. There was soot in the nasal passages and in his mouth. His eyes were reddened, he also had a hoarse cough. His breathing was elevated as was the depth of his respirations."

"Was there something missing that precluded a diagnosis of smoke inhalation?"

Gesturing toward her own throat, Hannah said, "He did not have any upper airway obstruction caused by swelling. Nor did he have any postural adaptations to suggest respiratory distress."

The attorney stopped pacing and looked at her with a puzzled expression. "Postural adaptations? Can you please explain what that means?"

"He did not appear to be positioning his body to make his breathing easier. This usually happens in more severe cases of smoke inhalation, when the lungs and bronchial tubes are damaged by the smoke and heat."

"So, overall, what was your assessment?"

"The dog had been suffering malnutrition and lack of adequate exercise. He showed some signs of having been breathing in the smoke from the wildfire for a while, but did not seem, initially, to have any acute injuries to his lungs or upper respiratory tract."

"The dog stayed with you for how long? Did any other signs or symptoms of injury show up during that time?"

"Three days." She refolded her hands in her lap. "He developed a deep, hoarser cough that suggested he had in fact had some mild irritation of the lungs and respiratory airways but nothing to the extent of full-blown smoke inhalation. Also, during that time, I was able to re-examine the dog. I found some other clues as to his state of health."

"What were they, please?"

Hannah held out a hand, fingers straight and splayed. "Toby had exceptionally long nails. No one was doing nail clippings on the dog. Also, both ears were infected with mites. We clipped his nails and started him on a regime of medications to rid him of the ear mites."

"Is there anything else you would like to add, doctor?"

"We still don't know about any previous veterinary care of the dog. If Mr. Malin were having the dog seen by someone, we would like to know about that so we can check the records for state required vaccinations, such as rabies."

"Thank you, Doctor Woodbridge for your testimony."

The defense attorney got up to cross-exam Hannah. He walked over to the witness stand and stood directly beside it. "Hello, Doctor Woodbridge. Thank you for coming today. You said in your testimony that your examination of Toby revealed signs of neglect. Is that true?"

"Yes, I believe it is true, that the dog was showing signs of neglect."

BID TO LOVE

"What were they again?"

"His nails were overgrown and he had ear mites. He was also underweight for the type of dog that he is, and his musculature was minimum at best. The dog has not been getting enough exercise."

The defense attorney looked at the finger nails of his own hand. "How much should a lab and pit bull crossbred dog weigh doctor?"

Hannah sat up straighter. "Well, a male Labrador retriever usually weighs anywhere from sixty-five to seventy-nine pounds, while a pit bull usually weighs from thirty-five to sixty-five pounds."

"So, the dog's weight was in the appropriate range for a pit bull but not a Labrador retriever, is that fair to say?" The attorney paced over to the judge's stand.

"Yes, and the dog had more genetic features of a Labrador than a pit bull, so I would expect the weight to be more in the weight range of a retriever than a pit bull."

Clasping his hands behind his back, the defense attorney asked, "How is Toby doing now?"

"He's doing well now, his hoarse cough has gone," Hannah answered, her hands tightly folded together in her lap.

"Have his ear mites cleared up?"

"Yes, the ear mites have cleared up."

"Has Toby's weight changed at all since his admission into the shelter?"

"He has gained three pounds in the last week. I expect, with the right amount of food and proper nutrition, he'll be putting on more weight in the coming weeks," Hannah smiled.

"Weeks? Do you expect he'll be in the shelter for weeks?"

"I expect that whoever has possession of the dog will continue to provide him with the appropriate amount of food and water. I will want to check him on a weekly basis until his weight gain tapers off."

Rocking back on his heels, the attorney said, "No further questions for the doctor, your honor."

DIANA ROCK

Lastly, Myron Malin was called to the stand.

CHAPTER TWENTY-FIVE

Sporting a rumpled, buffalo plaid shirt and well-worn and lightly stained jeans, Myron Malin was sworn in and sat in the witness chair just as Hannah and Andrew had done before him. He smoothed his trembling hand over his disheveled hair, the yellowed fingernails of his rough, calloused hands evident in the bright fluorescent lights of the courtroom.

Comparing how he looked now with his court appearance just months ago, Hannah was surprised how quickly his appearance had deteriorated. Remembering what Andrew had said about Mr. Malin's history of alcoholism, she said a prayer he would find his way back to sobriety soon.

She also noticed the look of defiance in his eyes. Despite his unkempt appearance, he looked confident. Considering he had won the last case Andrew had brought against him, he probably thought this hearing would also end with a win. Hannah feverishly hoped, for Toby's sake, that Mr. Malin would be wrong.

The defense attorney started the questioning.

"Mr. Malin, you have heard the testimony of Officer Kelly and Doctor Woodbridge. Would you like to explain what happened on the twenty-sixth of August?"

"Yup I would. I was at the local bar, having a lunch break. And I sees on the TV news that there's a wildfire burning, oh, about a half mile from my trailer."

"Did you try to go to your trailer?"

"No."

The attorney gestured with his hands. "Why not?"

"They said on the TV that the area roads was closed to traffic. I couldn't have gotten back to the trailer," Myron said, clutching the railing of the witness stand.

"You never went back to the trailer?"

"I did the next morning. The fire had skirted around that trailer park, so the trailers weren't damaged or destroyed. But Toby was gone."

A sad look on his face, the defense attorney asked, "What did you do?"

Myron replied, "I called the Animal Control Office to report him missing."

"Who took your call and what was said?"

"Don't know who took my call. I was told they had rescued the dog from the trailer, and it was at the veterinary clinic."

"Did he say anything else?"

"He said he was going to keep care of Toby until this hearing. He was going to file for custody of the dog again." Myron wrung his hands together.

"How did that make you feel, Mr. Malin?"

Myron scowled. "I was angry. I wanted Toby back."

"Did you know that dog had been injured by the smoke?"

"No, there was no mention of his having any injuries," Myron Malin said, with a surprised look on his face.

"Mr. Malin, you've heard the testimony of Doctor Hannah Woodbridge. She testified that the dog is undernourished and under exercised. There are also some care issues, such as the length of his nails and ear mites that required medication. Where you aware of these issues, Mr. Malin?"

Shaking his head, Myron said, "No. I've been feeding that dog good. Sure, he doesn't get a whole lotta exercise. Most the time, he's sitting or lying down under that trailer, in the shade. I try to take him for walks, but he won't come out from under that trailer."

"And the nails and ear mites?"

"I'm not real good at having the dog's nails trimmed. Can't do it by myself and I don't have the kind of spare change to get someone else to do it for me. I live on a fixed income. Didn't even know about the ear mites, whatever they are."

"When did you hear about the injuries due to the smoke inhalation."

"Just now. No one told me anything about my poor Toby. He's been locked up at the clinic and now at the shelter. I went to see him, but he was so scared he didn't even know who I was when I went there." Again, the man scowled, as if remembering how the dog refused to come when he called him.

"Mr. Malin, do you think you are a good caregiver for the dog?"

"Yes. I buy him food he likes; he gobbles it up fast. And I make sure he's got water. And he's got the shade of the trailer there to keep him cool."

"How about veterinary care? When was the last time Toby had his vaccines and what did he have?"

"Oh, I don't remember all that. I took him to the vet not too long ago. Must have been just a year or so because you have to have a valid rabies certificate to get 'em licensed. I remember it cost me a small fortune to take him there." Myron reached forward, his forefinger stabbing at the railing to reinforce his point.

The prosecution took over the questioning once the defense had finished.

"Mr. Malin, you said you heard on the TV that the roads to the trailer park were closed, is that correct?"

"Yes, sir."

"Knowing that you couldn't get to back to the trailer, did you do anything to alert someone that the dog was still at the trailer? Did you call the police or animal control to have them rescue your dog?"

Myron shook his head. "No, didn't think of that. I thought if I couldn't get through on the roads, nobody else could either."

"Did you know the dog license had expired?"

"No, I didn't."

"In fact, the license tag attached to the collar was registered by someone else, not by you. Why was that?"

"I got the dog from a friend. He came with the license and tag."

"Toby, came from your friend with a license and tag? Is that correct?"

Myron squirmed in his chair a few seconds. "Yes, sir, I did say that. That's the truth."

"But you never updated the license with your information. Why is that?"

"I didn't realize I had to."

"It's the law, sir." The lawyer stopped before the witness bench and tapped his index finger on his lips before asking, "Is it possible Mr. Malin, that you knew if you tried to get the dog licensed in your own name that you would not be able to do so because of your previous conviction for animal abuse and neglect?"

Mr. Malin's face flashed with anger before he looked down at his hands in his lap and mashed his lips together.

Sensing a small victory, the prosecuting attorney changed topic. "What is the name of the veterinarian you used last time you had Toby get his vaccines?"

Looking up, Mr. Malin thought a moment before saying, "I don't remember."

"Was it someone here in Colby or in a surrounding town?"

"It weren't anybody around here. A pet store in Mifflin, I think. They have a vet come and give out vaccines for cheap."

"I see, did you realize the dog might need a new set of vaccines, each year."

"Didn't give it much thought," he said, shaking his head again. "Toby's usually out of sight so he's out of mind, most of the time."

"I have no further questions for Mr. Malin, your honor."

Both the prosecution and the defense rested their case after Mr. Malin's testimony. Judge Shapiro retired to his chamber to deliberate on the case.

BID TO LOVE

Sitting in the back of the courtroom, Hannah observed the two groups of people at the front of the room. The two people at the defense table, Mr. Malin and his attorney, sat at either end of the table, silent and engaged in their own activities. The lawyer's nose was glued to his cell phone, Mr. Malin sat with his arms crossed over his chest and his eyes closed as if napping.

The prosecution table also had two people: Andrew and the town's attorney. Both were engaged in a thoughtful discussion. A third person, in the front row was consulted by the town's attorney. This woman must be the Desmond's law advocate Andrew had told her was working on the case with them. While she observed the discussion, Andrew glanced over at her, giving her a wink, before turning back to the attorney.

She felt her heart leap in her chest at the surprise wink across the empty courtroom. He had wiggled his way into her heart, with his sincere crusade for animals and animal rights. She prayed justice would be done today. It would crush him to lose Toby yet another time. But she knew even if the case were lost, Andrew would not give up on Toby. If anything, it would make him even more determined to save the dog from the chain attached to the back bumper of the trailer.

Would she be around to see it? If the bid selection didn't change, if Bryan Plat remained town veterinarian, she likely wouldn't be able to buy the vet clinic. Where would she go? What would she do? And as frightening as all that was for her right now, the thought of moving away and never seeing Andrew caused tears to well in her eyes. She blinked rapidly, trying to clear them away without wiping. The last think she wanted anyone in this room to see was her having an unprofessional emotional breakdown.

The sounds of doors opening, shifted her attention to the bailiff and judge returning with a verdict.

"Based on the testimony presented I am believe the dog in question, Toby, was not being properly cared for to the point of neglect.

This is upheld with the information that Mr. Malin did nothing at all to try to save Toby from the fire. I am ruling in favor of the prosecution. The Town of Colby will retain custody of the dog known to this court as Toby until he can be placed in a responsible home. Mr. Malin, your name will remain on a list of offenders. In the future, you will not be able to buy *or* be given a dog. This case is closed."

Andrew held the courthouse door open for Hannah, their arms brushing as she walked past. A warmth spread through her body from the touch. Despite the fact it had been weeks since their intimate encounter and she was still angry with him about backing Bryan Plat, she couldn't help the way her body seemed to melt near him. She glanced over at Andrew's face only to find him watching her, as they walked to the ACO van.

"What?"

"Nothing," Andrew replied with a smile that made her heart skip a beat.

Stopping beside the driver's door, Hannah said, "I thought my heart was going to leap out of my chest when the judge ruled in Toby's favor."

Andrew took her hand. "I know what you mean. I don't think I breathed until he declared Toby free." He smoothed his thumb over the back of her fingers as he spoke.

The surge swept through her body again. "Thanks to you, Toby is free," she said, giving his hand a squeeze.

"I couldn't have done it without you." Andrew closed the distance between them, taking her breath away.

Hannah felt the pull of his eyes on her lips. He was going to kiss her. A shiver ran down her spine and her heart stuttered. Her arms ached to wind themselves around his neck and pull him close. Despite what Andrew had done, she still felt the strong attraction between them. There was no denying it. Yet, there was a time and a place for such displays of affection. Not wanting him to kiss her outside in a public parking lot, she sidled away from him.

Andrew let go of her hand as she moved away. He frowned. "I'm sorry," he said, his eyes full of remorse.

"Just — not here," Hannah explained. Glancing around, they stood beside the van in awkward silence.

Breaking the silence, Hannah offered, "Why don't we go to my place for some coffee?"

"I'll have to stop at the shelter to feed the guests first." Andrew replied. "See you in little bit."

CHAPTER TWENTY-SIX

The smell of freshly brewed coffee and a plate of Girl Scout cookies were waiting when Andrew arrived at Hannah's apartment.

Hannah poured two mugs while Andrew greeted Maggie. With the fireplace going, the living room was warm and cozy. And romantic. They sat on the sofa, Maggie Mae at their feet. Andrew slung his arm around Hannah's shoulders and nestled her into the crook of his arm. *It's going to be okay.*

"I'm glad it's over," Hannah said just before taking another bite of a minty cookie.

"Me too. I'm glad it's finally over. And we won." Andrew set down his mug and reached for his fourth cookie.

"So," Hannah perked, "Now you have to find Toby a new home."

Andrew nodded, "I know, I know. I must find someone incredibly special to take that dog. I don't want to hand him over to just anyone. Toby deserves an exceptional home, where I know he'll be taken care of properly and diligently. We owe it to him to do that. He has a lot of time left in the shelter so we can wait for the right person."

"I have an idea."

"What's that?"

"Well, I took on Maggie Mae when push came to shove. How about you taking on Toby?"

Andrew frowned. "I can't do that. I'm gone all hours of the day and night."

"Take him with you. The dog needs exercise and socialization. What better way than to become your right seat passenger?"

"Let me think about it. I don't know that the town will go for it, and they would have to approve."

The crunching of shortbread cookies filled the silence between them.

"Did I tell you I have a new niece?" Andrew blurted.

Hannah picked up her coffee again. "No, you didn't. Congratulations, Uncle Andrew." She smiled at the idea. "I'll bet you look cute with a baby in your arms."

Andrew looked at her before averting his eyes. "It's the closest I'll ever get to one."

Cupping the mug in both hands, Hannah cocked her head. "You don't ever expect to be a father?"

"Can't," he whispered, his eyes fixed on his plate.

Warm coffee spilt out of her trembling mug as Hannah set it back down on the table. She stared at him, wishing him to say more as she reached for a napkin. Explain more. Instead, he continued to clean his plate and drink his coffee, his eyes averted.

What can I say? What do you say to something like that? That it doesn't matter? Clearly it does to him. And he clearly did not want to talk about the issue anymore.

CHAPTER TWENTY-SEVEN

They were silent a few minutes both staring into the bottom of their mugs.

Andrew set down his cup and pulled her chin up to look at him. Hannah peered through the fringe of her long lashes to see him eye to eye. He bent over and brushed his lips over hers. They were soft and pliable. She kissed him back sweetly.

Hannah whispered as he pulled back several inches, "I never thought I'd have a friend with benefits."

Andrew stiffened slightly, putting more distance between their lips. "I think we are for the sake of necessity. Once you've won the contract, I hope that we can be more than just friends with benefits."

Hannah blinked, sitting up straight, pulling out of the circle of his arm. "Do you mean, you're keeping your distance publicly until you're sure I've won the contract?"

Andrew raked his hand through his hair. "You have to admit it would be awkward if anyone suspected the reason you won it was because you were my girlfriend. It is better that we keep it low key until that whole issue is settled."

"I'm a lot surprised you even thought of such things." Hannah sat up stiffly.

"Hey, I'm not a macho-he-man. I care about you and how it might look. I want to make sure you win the contract on your own reputation and experience rather than muck up the works with me in the picture."

"What if Bryan Plat keeps the contract?" Hannah felt her blood starting to heat to a steaming point, as she thought about Andrew's previous desire to have Bryan win. Knowing about their true relationship, a fact Andrew had still failed to mention, made it even hotter.

"Once it's settled, one way or another, I will be here for you." Andrew said.

"One way or another? Are you kidding me?" she snapped, feeling her blood pressure sky rocket.

"Yes, I mean, no, it doesn't matter to me with regard to our relationship. But it has to be settled."

She didn't know what to make of the statement. Did he think she would thank him for respecting her reputation? For putting their relationship on hold? Or should she be pissed off that he would let the situation interfere? Wouldn't it be more romantic of him to have damned the situation and pursued her anyway?

Hannah bolted from the sofa and paced the living room, one palm holding her forehead.

"What's wrong? Did I say something wrong?" Andrew asked, standing up, grasping her forearm.

She shook him off. "I'm not sure. But I think you should go." Hannah said to him over her shoulder.

Andrew ran his fingers through his hair again. "Hannah, I —"

"Just go, please," she said, pointing to the door. "I need to think."

Andrew stared at her a moment, pain and confusion filling his eyes. He stooped to give Maggie Mae a pat on the head as he walked by her. Hannah watched him go, watched him stop at her apartment door and turn around.

"You know where I am if you want to talk." Andrew said before turning on his heels and closing the door behind him.

Hannah bolted the door. Slumping against it, she closed her eyes and tried to get the look in his eyes out of her mind. He looked hurt. She had hurt him with her confusion. What was the issue? What rankled her so much that she'd thrown him out of the apartment? She wanted him to come clean. And there was no indication he would. He doled out information in bits and pieces as if not trusting her with the full story. How long did he think he could hide it from her? What did that mean given the intimacy they shared?

Stomping over to the coffee table she picked up her mug and drained it. "What in have I done?"

***

Outside in the driveway, Andrew sat behind the wheel of his car, looking at Hannah's window. How much of her reaction was about his revelation? He hadn't meant to blurt out anything about his sterility. It had spilt out without warning or design.

His gut ached with the realization that this might be the end of them. If she wanted children in her future like he suspected she did, he'd nixed their relationship with his "can't" confession. Would telling her more, telling her why make it any better? The heaviness in his chest failed to offer any hope.

With a sigh he started the car. As he pulled way, his head told him what his heart already knew. He loved her. He needed her in his life. More importantly, he'd blown it with one careless word.

CHAPTER TWENTY-EIGHT

Hannah received a letter requesting her presence along with the other bidders at a special meeting of the Bid Selection Committee. No mention was made of the reason though Hannah knew exactly what it was. Held in the same room, Hannah sat by herself, in the same seat as before. Her sweating hands clenched together in her lap, she tried to remain as calm as possible. *This is going to be it.* She thought. *This is going to either make me or break me, once and for all on more levels than one.*

Hannah thought of Andrew and the words they had shared during their last meeting. He had said "one way or another" but did he really mean it? And how would she feel about him if she lost the bid a second time? Then she remembered it was he who had pointed out the requirements of the winning bidder setting this reconsideration in motion. Surely, he had to be on her side if he had gone to the trouble of exposing those requirements. She glanced over her shoulder at him. Andrew sat alone instead of with his former pal, Bryan Plat, on the side of the hall, as though he were merely a by-stander to the event. Hannah centered her focus back on the front table as the committee members began to assemble.

Paul Tabs and Bryan Plat arrived at the same time, shaking hands briefly. Doctor Tabs took a seat in the same area he had sat during the last meeting. Bryan sat beside Andrew, but Andrew got up and moved to another seat across the room. Bryan scowled.

Mayor Analis was the last to arrive. She walked in with a tall, corporate-suited gentleman, the attorney who had worked the second Malin case with Andrew. The gentleman took a seat to the side of the hall. Once she had taken her seat at the center of the table and organized some papers before her, the mayor began the meeting.

"Thank you all, for coming to this meeting of the selection committee. I'd like to introduce the town's attorney, Arthur Chandler."

She indicated the gentleman who had walked in with her. He gave the audience a brisk nod before Mayor Analis continued. "Some important information has been brought to our attention and this information has a bearing on the selection committee's decision in awarding the Town of Colby contract for veterinary services for the Animal Control Program."

Bryan Plat jumped up. "I was awarded the contract. I don't see what more needs to be looked into."

Mayor Analis waved him to sit down. "I'm going to explain the entire situation in a moment. Please be so kind as to take your seat."

Slowly, begrudgingly, Bryan sat down again, glaring at the front table, then at Andrew.

"It was brought to our attention that the wording of the bidding requirements indicates that the winning bidder shall remain within the Town of Colby boundaries while providing the duties set forth in the contract. The only remedy for this is for a qualified backup to be provided during those times when the contract winner is not within town limits." The mayor looked at each of the bidders as she spoke, making eye contact.

"The selection committee has consulted with Mr. Chandler and he has looked at the wording of the passage and agrees with the interpretation. So, the winning bidder, must then provide twenty-four hour/three sixty-five-day service or make arrangements with another qualified veterinarian to cover."

Bryan vaulted up again, interrupting. "That's ridiculous. There's no reason you should require that kind of service. I don't see why I would need to remain within the city limits of the town for the duration of the coverage. My office is only four miles from the town line."

"Sit down, Doctor Plat. This meeting is not about the necessity of the type of coverage. It is only to examine the bidding requirements," the mayor explained. "The fact remains, the request for bids stipulates this in-town coverage be provided by the winning bidder."

Bryan Platt sat, shaking his head.

The mayor continued speaking, "Furthermore, the wording of the duties reads that the winning bidder will help write regulations with regard to animal welfare within the town. That in itself is not the issue. The issue is that town statutes require that anyone involved in the writing of town regulations must be a resident of the town of Colby. Thus, the bid winner, must also live within the town of Colby."

Doctor Plat jumped up again, blurting out, "This is absurd. There is no reason that I should have to be a citizen of Colby in order to provide substantive influence on the writing of regulations for the health and welfare of animals within the town."

The mayor waved him to sit down again. "Doctor Plat, I have asked you repeatedly to remain seated. Please refrain from speaking until after I am finished presenting the committee's findings or I'll ask you to leave."

Bryan Plat slapped his thigh with his hand before resuming his seat, muttering under his breath the entire time and shooting Andrew a tortuous look.

"As I was saying," the mayor continued, "unfortunately, the town statutes do require it. Again, we have checked with our attorney on the interpretation of the regulation and it has been agreed. The bid winner must reside in Colby."

"Based on this enlightened information, the Bid Selection Committee is rescinding our contract award to Doctor Plat. The doctor neither lives nor works within the boundaries of the town of Colby."

Bryan Plat jumped up again, but the mayor continued. "In fact, of the three bidders, only one meets the qualifications for both issues. Doctor Woodbridge is the only bidding veterinarian who works *in* the town and *is* a resident in the town of Colby. Based on this information, the selection committee is awarding the contract for veterinary services for the Animal Control Program to Doctor Hannah Woodbridge. Congratulations, Doctor Woodbridge," said Mayor Analis.

Doctor Plat turned around and glared at Hannah, his mouth busy muttering what she guessed was foul language; unintelligible to her from across the room.

Everyone else in the room had also turned to look at Hannah. Jubilant, but trying to remain calm, she chose to remain seated, unsmiling lest anyone mistake her smile for a smirk.

Out of the corner of her eye, Hannah watched as Bryan Plat stormed toward her. She got to her feet, steeling herself for another verbal assault. But before he could get to her, Andrew had caught Bryan by the upper arm and halted him in his tracks. The two men glared at each other for a second. As Hannah watched, Andrew said something to Bryan. In return, Bryan scowled before turning on his heels and stalking out of the room.

When he was sure Bryan had left, Andrew glanced over to Hannah and gave her a nod.

Hannah smiled back at him and nodded, before being interrupted by Mayor Analis for a congratulatory handshake.

Hannah walked to her car alone. While she was ecstatic about winning the bid, a hollowness in her chest prevailed. She had hoped Andrew would have said something to her, congratulated her maybe. But he hadn't. Caught up in an animated conversation with the police chief, he'd looked preoccupied with another matter. Too preoccupied to speak with her. And she had run out of reasons to stick around. *Go ahead and miss him all you want. You did this to yourself. You threw him out of your apartment. Idiot!*

"Hey. Wait up a minute."

She stopped and turned around to see Andrew jogging toward her. Her heart started keeping pace with the sound of his footfalls on the asphalt. He drew up in front of her and held out his hand. "Congratulations."

Hannah shook his hand and smiled broadly. "Thanks. Thanks to your encouragement, I won the bid."

"I'd kiss you but there are still too many eyes in this parking lot," Andrew said, glancing over his shoulder.

There he was again. Afraid to be seen out in public with her. She gave it a few seconds thought, feeling her face flush and the heat rising in the rest of her body as she thought of being so near to him. "We should call it a night. Besides, you don't want to be seen with me."

"Let's not discuss this here," he said. "Still have that bottle of Scotch at your apartment? Care to share a glass?"

Hannah's mind and heart went aflutter. Andrew had helped her win back the contract. Maybe the distance he'd put between them had helped. It certainly could not have hurt the case. "Yeah, come on then. Meet me at my apartment."

"I have the van. Let me go get my own vehicle from the shelter. I'll meet you at your place in about twenty."

CHAPTER TWENTY-NINE

Twenty-two minutes later, Hannah opened her apartment door to a refreshed Andrew Kelly. No longer dressed in the uniform of his Animal Control Office, he was decked out in a pair of snug fitting jeans and a jersey top that hugged his toned torso. Over the jersey he wore a dark brown leather jacket. The overall look was very European and sexy as hell. Hannah couldn't take her eyes off him.

"Aren't you going to ask me to come in?" he asked sheepishly. "I dressed extra special for our celebration." Maggie Mae ran circles around his ankles, panting and whining for his attention as he stood there, his entire attention on Hannah.

"Come in," Hannah said, backing away from the open doorway to let Andrew in. "If I had known you were getting so dressed up for the occasion, I would have put on something more comfortable."

"Don't let me stop you," he replied. "You look uncomfortable in that pants suit."

Andrew walked into the living room of Hannah's apartment and sat on the sofa. Maggie settled on the floor beside his feet. The gas fireplace was going, and only one lamp was lit in the room, illuminating the room in a romantic ambiance. Hannah waited by the coffee table. "You still want that drink?"

"If that Glen Grant Scotch is still on the menu, I'd love a couple fingers worth."

Hannah went into the small galley kitchen, pulled out the bottle of 30-year-old Scotch and poured two glasses. Remembering how he liked it last time, she dropped one ice cube into each glass. She brought both glasses, setting them on the coffee table before Andrew and taking a seat beside him.

Holding up his glass, Andrew said, "To Doctor Hannah Woodbridge, Town of Colby Veterinarian."

Gripping her glass, Hannah clinked it with Andrew's then took a sip. The warm liquid was smooth and decadent across her tongue and down her throat as she swallowed. She breathed in the aroma and closed her eyes. It smelled delicious and tasted great. The perfect way to celebrate her victory over adversity. She opened her eyes and looked into Andrew's. "If you hadn't crashed my pity-party and made me examine the application details, I never would have won the contract back."

Andrew waved his near empty glass in the air, "Ah, it was nothing really. I'm glad you won, Hannah."

They sat still, Andrew resting his head on top of Hannah's, his arms around her waist. She gently turned his chin. "I think you're a wonderful guy, Andrew Kelly. Even if I was your second choice."

Andrew stared into her eyes. "I was a fool, Hannah. You'll always be my first choice, forever more."

Glancing away, Hannah let go of Andrew's chin and was silent. *Does he mean it? Can he really be saying he's on my side now? Can I trust him to stay on my side?* Andrew broke the ice. "So, you're inviting me here must mean you're feeling okay now."

"Okay about what?" Hannah asked, taking a slip of Scotch.

"Well, last time I was here, you pretty much threw me out. Nicely, but nonetheless, you told me to leave."

"I'm still not sure on that account. I felt like celebrating, but not alone," Hannah said.

"So, you're still sore at me?"

"I haven't decided yet."

"All this time and you still haven't decided yet?" Andrew set down his glass. "Is there another reason you asked me to leave, Hannah?"

"No, no. Look, between work and getting ready for the bid selection, I've been going flat out most of the time. My only down time has been walking Maggie Mae."

"But you must have some feelings about what I told you," Andrew persisted.

Hannah set down her glass this time and put her hands in her lap. "I'm grateful you thought enough of me to want to protect my reputation." *Dare I go there?* "But I think there's more to this story than you're letting on."

Andrew closed his eyes and sighed heavily. Silently, he walked over to the window and stared out into the night. Turning around he cleared his throat. "Um, there's a couple things." He swallowed hard. "I used to work for Bryan. Up until five years ago, when I took the ACO job. He hired me right out of vet tech school."

Hannah crossed her arms over her chest but said nothing. This was no surprise to her either. He had told her this before.

"He helped me get the ACO job." Andrew ran his fingers through his hair. "Hell, he paid for all the classes at the Academy I needed so I could even be eligible for the job. He knew the ACO at the time was going to be retiring. He talked the guy into holding out until I was ready to apply for the job." Andrew walked over and sat down beside Hannah on the sofa. He angled his body to face her.

"When I worked for Bryan, I introduced him to my sister, Kimberly. All the while I was going to classes, Bryan and Kim were dating. Not long after I got this job, they married." He looked Hannah square in the eyes. "Bryan is my brother-in-law."

Hannah finally spoke. "Is that why you backed him for the job?"

Andrew hung his head. "At first, yes. That, and I felt like I owed him. God, I still owe him thousands of dollars for all my classes. He also bent over backward to give me a work schedule that fit my class schedule. And then there's my sister, of course. She wants a cruise on the Mediterranean. Bryan wanted the money for that." He looked up into her eyes. "And I didn't *know you* in the beginning. I didn't have faith in you."

He stood and paced to the window again. "Once I got to know you, how competent you are, my feelings changed. But I couldn't shake off my promise to back Bryan. And I knew it wouldn't look good either way. So I just stayed as far away from the decision-making process as possible."

He sat back down beside her. "You understand I was trying to help you in the end? I didn't want any hint of our relationship to interfere. That's all it was, Hannah. Me trying to help you. To give you a fair chance. I didn't want anything to stand in the way." Andrew took Hannah's hand from her lap and held it in his warm palm.

"I appreciate that. I guess I wanted someone to want *me* and not give two hoots about the rest of the world."

Andrew was silent a moment. "So, you're saying you wouldn't have cared if you lost the bid because you were sleeping with me?"

"No, that's not what I'm saying. Well — maybe it is what I'm saying. But I desperately needed that contract. Going without it would ruin me."

"Is it really that important?"

"Yeah. The bank wouldn't give me the loan to buy the clinic business from Doc Cambria unless I got the appointment. If I didn't get the loan, I'd have to leave Colby."

"Why?" Andrew's eyes flew wide open at her admission.

"Doc Cambria is selling the practice. I was his first choice. But if I can't buy it, someone else will."

The pained expression on his face waned. "Then I'm awfully glad I thought to try to keep my distance long enough to ensure you got the contract fair and square. And I'm equally glad you won it back from Bryan." Andrew squeezed her hand again.

He cocked his head and looked at her sheepishly before he continued. "Regarding the other confession I made."

A puzzled look registered on Hannah's face.

"During dinner when I said I can't father children."

Hannah's eyes widened but she remained silent.

"When I was a child I had surgery. It was a complicated bilateral hernia repair. In the area of the vas deferens, those tubes that carry the sperm from testicles to, well, outside. The tubes got damaged, either from the surgery or from scar tissue." He swallowed hard, his eyes sad. "I'm sterile."

Giving his hand a squeeze back, Hannah replied, "That's not so bad. I mean, if your body is still producing sperm but they can't get out, there are other ways."

Slowly, Andrew nodded. "Perhaps. But making children isn't going to be an easy process with me. And most every woman dreams of having children."

"Well I'm not one of them."

Andrew's mouth dropped open. He remained soundless for a few seconds. "You never played with dolls or dreamed of the children you would have and what you would name them?"

Blushing violently, Hannah shook her head. "While my girlfriends were playing house with dolls, I was playing vet with stuffed animals. And my dreams were of the pets I would have and what I would name them."

"So, you never even thought of having a family?"

"By the time I hit high school, I was too busy studying to even consider anything beyond vet school." Hannah shrugged. "I really haven't had time to stop and consider things like buying a house, getting married, and having a family."

"But you're not opposed to the idea?"

"Heavens no." Tilting her head she glared at him with an odd expression on her face. "Andrew Kelly, did you think I broke it off with you because you said you couldn't father children?"

He shrugged one shoulder and gave her a lopsided smile. "Guilty."

"Come closer." She leaned toward him and stared straight into his eyes. "That is the least of my concerns. What bothered me was you keeping secrets."

"No more secrets." He stretched forward and touched his lips to hers. Their softness filled Hannah with longing. Then the kiss changed as a hunger seemed to overtake him. He ran his fingers into her hair and pulled her forward, his tongue searching for hers. Hannah let hers play with his, reveling in the taste of Scotch as they played. The pounding of her heart sounded so loud she thought surely, he could hear it.

Struggling to his feet without breaking contact, Andrew took Hannah into his arms and crushed her against him. A sharp pang of desire swept through her. The points of her breasts hardened against his rock-hard chest. She felt a growing ache at the apex of her thighs. And she felt the hardness of him through the thin fabric of her pants.

"God, Hannah, you are exquisite," Andrew said.

Hannah couldn't think of anything to say. Instead, she took Andrew by the hand and led him beyond her bedroom door. Leaving Maggie Mae to guard the apartment by herself.

CHAPTER THIRTY

Toby stayed at the shelter. During that time, he had been the roaming mascot in the Animal Control Office, just as Maggie Mae had been before him. For socialization, Andrew regularly took the dog out with him, especially when they were to meet up with Hannah and Maggie at the dog park. The two dogs became fast buddies, playing and romping and chasing balls together.

They were standing inside the perimeter of the fenced dog park, watching Maggie tussle with another dog for a stick late one October afternoon. Toby sat between Hannah and Andrew, panting and watching the scuffle; seemingly happier to be beside them. "He's such a happier dog outside the shelter." Hannah said of their many dates with the dogs.

"Yes, I have noticed. I'd be too if it were me."

Hannah bent down to Toby as she scratched the center of his head. "He's your guardian angel, you know that boy, don't you?"

Andrew's breath hitched as the gaping low-cut shirt collar exposed her breasts. He was always struck by her natural beauty, but more so today as she gazed lovingly at the dog. Without makeup, her skin glowed as she stroked Toby's head, the dog peering up at her with adoration in his eyes. Andrew knew that sentiment.

Standing up, Hannah added, "I can't understand why no one has adopted him yet. He's such a happy dog."

"I have no clue what keeps people from picking him. Though he's still on the skinny side, I always mention he's recovering from a neglect situation."

Andrew pulled a ball out of his pocket and showed it to Toby. The dog responded by leaping at it. "No boy, down." When the dog sat at his feet, Andrew threw the ball across the park. Toby gave chase before retrieving it and dropping it at Andrew's feet.

BID TO LOVE

"You've been watching over him now for a while. Don't you think it's time to make it official?"

Andrew rough-housed with the dog, then picked up his ball and threw it across the park again. As he watched, a warm feeling spread through his bones as he thought of adopting Toby himself. "Maybe you're right. I am quite fond of him. He's a loving dog and a fast learner. He's learned all the commands quickly. He was well trained."

"You know, I didn't think I was ready for Maggie Mae either, but since the moment she came into my life, she's been a blessing." Hannah put her hand on his forearm and looked him in the eye. "Consider taking the plunge, Andrew."

The warm feeling grew into excitement as he seriously considered taking Toby home for good. No more lonesome nights. They could watch TV together. He'd have a fishing pal. And someone to greet him when he came home from work unless he decided to bring him along to work. As he thought of all these things, the feelings grew stronger, and he knew Hannah was right. Adopting Toby would be a blessing for both of them.

"Okay, okay. I'll fill out the paperwork and pay the bill. I'll take him home tonight."

Clapping her hands together, Hannah jumped up and down, grinning broadly. "That's great!"

After their date in the dog park, Andrew took Toby back to the office. He filled out the adoption papers and wrote a check for his new best friend. Then they went to the pet store to get all the supplies they would need to keep, feed, and house the dog under his roof. Andrew was surprised how much it cost when he checked out, he'd bought a lot of extra things — a new collar and leash set, a big dog bed, water and food bowls, food and treats, and toys. Lots of dog toys hit the shopping cart.

When he got home, he brought the dog into the house first, then brought in the food and water bowls and fed the dog his first meal as a free dog. A lump formed in his throat as he watched the dog eat. When he was done, Toby sat back on his haunches and stared around the kitchen with a smile on his face. Andrew left the dog alone for a few minutes to carry in the remaining items, setting the dog bed beside the couch. The pile of dog toys went beside the bed.

Once he was finished carrying all the items in, Andrew made himself a sandwich and sat at the kitchen table to eat it. Toby was sitting right there, waiting for a hand out. He even held up one paw to shake in exchange for a bite, but Andrew knew better than to give the dog table scraps. People food was for people and dog food was for dogs. Instead, he got up and went to the kitchen counter to get Toby's treat. As he turned back around to hand Toby the biscuit, he caught the last sight of his sandwich as it passed into the dog's mouth.

"Hey, boy, that was my sandwich!" Andrew said aloud, causing the dog to flinch and skitter away. Immediately he was sorry for speaking so abruptly and scaring the poor dog so much. He needed to be more aware that he now resided with a creature that had spent its life in fear.

Instead, Andrew made himself another sandwich, this time eating it entirely before getting up from the table. He popped open a beer and settled on the couch. Toby settled down in the dog bed beside the couch.

As he sat there drinking his beer, Hannah's words reverberated in his brain. "Consider taking the plunge, Andrew," she had said. She was so beautiful and loving. So very much a beautiful person inside and out. He didn't know what he would do without her in his life. Hell, he didn't know what he would do if he couldn't see her every day. And it struck him, suddenly, that he couldn't let her slip through his fingers. Not now, not ever. He loved her. Andrew felt his heart rejoice at the thought of having Hannah with him always. With her, he didn't fear a toxic marriage like his parents had. Or a nasty divorce. He knew they would make it. They communicated well and understood each other far better than Kimberly and Bryan ever had. And she wasn't afraid of his infertility issue. If they decided they wanted children, they would deal with the issue together. If it worked out, great. If not, they would still have each other and she would be enough for him, he decided.

He knew what he had to do.

***

Andrew knocked on his sister and brother-in-law's front door. Despite still wearing his comfortable work uniform, he was stiff and itchy. He'd much rather be anywhere else. But he'd requested this meeting to get some important things off his chest.

The navy blue painted colonial wood door opened, Daniel scurrying out and hugging his legs. "Hey buddy, how are you today?" Andrew knelt down to talk directly to his godson. "Are you happy to see me?"

"Yes! Yes! Yes!" Daniel said, his still clenching Andrew's pants as he jumped up and down.

Kimberly appeared in the doorway, the baby slung up on her shoulder. "Daniel, let Uncle Andrew inside the house."

The child obeyed, taking his uncle's hand and leading him inside mini-mansion of a house in Westerville's best neighborhood. The richly furnished living room adjacent to the front foyer looked as though it had never been used.

The three joined Bryan in the dining room, Daniel nestled himself onto Andrew's lap while Bryan got Andrew a beer from the enormous side-by-side refrigerator in the adjacent granite and glass infused kitchen.

"Hey pal, I need to talk with your parents for a few minutes. Why don't you go to your room and play and I'll meet you there when we're done talking here?"

His big eyes glistened with tears as he slid off his uncle's lap. "Promise? I want to show you what I painted in school."

"I promise I'll come see what you painted in school. Okay?" Andrew soothed the child's hair before he scurried away.

"So, what's going on?" Kimberly asked after settling the baby in a seat.

"I need to talk with both of you about my future." He leaned forward, his hands folded on the table top.

Kimberly reached across the table, placing her hand over his. "Whatever is the matter, we will support you. You're my youngest brother. What's wrong? Is it cancer?"

He couldn't stop himself from rolling his eyes. "God, no. Nothing like that. Nothing medical. I am in love with someone, and I would like to be able to —" He faltered, not having actually prepared what he wanted to say he didn't know what to call it.

"Oh, are you going to get married?" Kimberly nearly squealed. She jumped up and down in her chair like a child.

"Not that far yet. But I would like to be able to include her in family gatherings and whatnot." He shrugged. "You know what I mean."

Kimberly rested back in her chair. "So, you want us to include her whenever we include you in something?"

Andrew glanced over at Bryan, who had remained silent, staring at his beer bottle during the entire conversation. *He's guessed already. He knows what I'm going to say and what I'm asking of him specifically.* "Yes, and I need you both to make her feel welcome."

"Well, what's her name?" Kimberly demanded, her smile enlightening her face.

"Hannah Woodbridge."

Kimberly's smile tensed and dimmed. "Do you mean the vet?"

"Yes he does." Bryan's voice boomed out as he scrapped back his chair and stalked back into the kitchen. He paused at the kitchen window and looked out.

Kimberly smiled briefly and glanced over her shoulder at her husband before adding. "I can do that. But I don't know that …"

Andrew felt the fury rising in his core. "Look. Either you include her and be nice or you lose me. But remember Daniel loses me too. And Erica."

"After what she did? You want me to socialize with her?" Bryan responded, his arms crossed over his chest stiffly, his lips so tight his words sounded clipped.

Andrew's blood pressure rising as he stood up. "After what *she* did? As I recall, you were the one who verbally attacked her. She never said a peep to you."

"She went back to the selection committee, and she got me revoked as the winner."

"She didn't do that. You got disqualified because you did not meet the specifications in the bid. She merely questioned. The selection committee decided the point she made was valid." Andrew walked over to stand in front of Bryan, but not in his personal space. "I know it badly bruises your ego to have a female win over you. But it was fair, and you are going to have to accept her as a part of my life. Maybe temporarily. Maybe long term."

Walking back to his sister, Andrew swung his arm around her shoulders, hugged her and kissed her cheek. "I'll go see Daniel now. You two can decide and let me know."

***

Barbra Pari was waiting outside Hannah's office one morning when she arrived at work. With a mischievous smile on her face, clutching a post-it note, she said, "Good morning!"

"What's going on?" Hannah asked, glancing around. "Is there some kind of joke or prank going on?" She fished her key out of her pocket, unlocked her door, and dumped her lunch bag and purse on her desk as she stepped in the room.

"I come bearing good news." Barbra leaned against the door jamb, cracking a wide smile.

"Well, out with it, please. I could use good news to start my day." Hannah shrugged off her light sweater and draped it over the back of her desk chair. She reached for her white coat.

"At first I thought it was a coincidence, but now I'm certain what I'm seeing is true." Barbra, held up the slip of paper. "Nearly all the clients that left our practice to go to Bryan Plat's have returned."

"Wow!" Hannah stopped mid-way putting on her coat. "Back to stay?"

"Sounds like it." Barbra said, folding her arms across her chest with a smug look on her face.

Hannah finished putting on her lab coat. "Did they give any hint why they're back?" She didn't much care what the reason was as long as the clientele was rising again.

"Every woman who offered an explanation said they heard how he treated you after the first bid selection award."

"Really? I wonder who is spreading that information about?" Hannah stuffed her stethoscope in her coat pocket,

"They didn't specify who is spreading the gossip. But they also said his prices were higher."

"Hmm, that's probably the truer cause of their return."

Barbra turned to leave. "Whatever, it's making the bottom line look great."

"Any chance we can add some hours to Doctor Stewart's contract?" Hannah gave a smug smile. "Assuming she'll want them, of course."

Laughing outright, Barbra nodded. "I think we can make that happen without a problem."

CHAPTER THIRTY-ONE

Hannah scanned the assembly. It was a beautiful Saturday afternoon in late October for the grand re-opening of the Colby County Veterinary Clinic under new ownership. The weather was warm and sunny, with cirrus clouds high aloft in the robin's egg blue sky. Eyes searching, she looked for one set of brown eyes in particular. There wasn't much of a crowd to witness the event — a mere thirty or so clients, some with their canines, not including the clinic staff. Several town dignitaries were in attendance, including Mayor Analis. Hannah's heart lightened when she caught sight of Andrew in the middle of the crowd. By his side sat Toby, whose nose was busy sniffing the behind of a nearby Irish setter. Andrew was preoccupied talking to the policeman beside him.

Feeling the jitter in her gut, she rocked back and forth on her feet, trying not to seem as tense as she was but needing to dispel some nervous energy. *Come on, let's get this over with.* Despite the fact that the loan papers and sale papers were signed already, she was on edge over this affair. She never really liked crowds and certainly didn't like being the center of attention of one.

Looking over her shoulder at the front of the clinic building, Hannah was once again amazed at how it had been decorated. Some of the vet technicians had made paper cutouts of cats and dogs and strung them together. They hung over the windows and over the lintels like Christmas garlands. Hannah made a mental note to save them for the Christmas season. They would make perfect decorations for the clinic's waiting room.

For the ribbon cutting ceremony, Barbra Pari had draped a ribbon of crepe paper across the main entrance to the clinic. Until the ceremony was completed, anyone coming or going from the building was directed to the back door. But there was little traffic. All appointment slots for the noon hour had been deliberately left empty. Everyone on staff had their fingers crossed there would be no emergency cases until the event concluded at half past. Either way, Doctor Cortland Stewart was on duty today to take care of them.

Applause broke out and grew as Doctor Cambria was wheeled up the ramp by his wife. The butterflies in Hannah's stomach jumped. *It was finally going to happen.* She couldn't wait to get away from the crowd, out of her high heels and back into her ballet flats — back to seeing her patients.

Doctor Cambria gave Hannah a wink as his wheelchair rolled past, his wife settling it to Hannah's right. The crowd waited quietly for the auspicious event of formally handing over the keys to the clinic to its new owner. Barbra Pari had rushed over to greet the doctor and his wife, saying a few words to them both. As Hannah looked on, Barbra gave Doctor Cambria a nod to begin whenever he was ready, then she took a place standing just behind Hannah.

It was to be a simple ceremony. Looking well, but still unable to move his left arm much, nor able to stand, Doctor Cambria began with a few words of welcome to the crowd.

"Thank you, everyone for coming. It's so good to see so many of you here today," he said, his voice quavering as he spoke as loudly as he could. Everyone listened carefully as there wasn't a microphone available. Even the dogs seemed to be on their best behavior as Doctor Cambria spoke of the clinic and his fond memories there. Finally, his wife gave him a little nudge on the shoulder to remind him that everyone was waiting for him to hand over the key.

Doctor Cambria raised his hands in surrender. "I digress about the good times. We are here today to welcome and transfer our beloved veterinary clinic to this delightful and competent veterinarian, Doctor Hannah Woodbridge."

Hannah looked out at the crowd of people who had come to celebrate with her. Her eyes caught and held on Andrew's, and he gave her a big smile as he nodded along with Doctor Cambria. A nudge from Barbra Pari brought her attention back to the moment. She stepped forward to stand beside Doctor Cambria who held out a shiny, silver key with his right hand.

"Doctor Woodbridge, I give you this key to the Colby County Veterinary Clinic and in so doing, transfer ownership of the building, all its contents, and all its responsibilities to you."

Hannah clasped the key with her left hand while shaking his right hand with her own. Her heart swelled with emotion and her eyes blurred with tears at the thought of finally reaching her goal of having her own veterinary clinic.

"Hold it." A photographer from the local paper stepped forward to take the picture for the next day's edition. The crowd cheered and dogs started barking with the noise.

Barbra Pari handed Hannah a pair of scissors. Hannah approached the clinic's front door, cut the crepe paper ribbon, then inserted the key in the door lock and opened it. Again, the crowd cheered.

As if on cue, four veterinary technicians began milling about the crowd carrying trays of cookies and paper cups of punch. The crowd of well-wishers swarmed forward to Hannah, shaking her hand, and congratulating her on her new venture. Hannah smiled brightly thanking people as they approached. Out of the corner of her eye, she saw Bryan Plat heading her way, with a woman carrying a baby at his side. At the woman's nudge, Bryan stepped forward.

Teeth clenching and knees locked rigid, she stood tall and silent.

"Dr. Woodbridge," he stopped in front of her before stiffly thrusting out his hand. "Congratulations."

Shaking it gingerly, Hannah said, "Thank you, Dr. Plat."

"I also want to apologize for my behavior at the bid meeting."

Hannah gave him a curt nod. "I accept your apology."

The woman stepped forward with a warm smile, juggling the baby in one arm while thrusting out a hand. "I'm Kimberly. His wife and Andrew's sister. I wanted to meet you and congratulate you on your success."

Smiling back, Hannah relaxed at her kindness and shook her hand. "Thank you. It's very nice to meet you."

Dressed in his uniform that accentuated his long lean form, Andrew walked over with Toby on a leash and a little boy beside him. Kimberly passed off the baby to him, taking the little boy's hand and the dog's leash. Andrew bounced and swayed as the baby stirred from her slumber.

Bobbing his head toward the little boy, Andrew said, "That's Daniel, my godson. And this is my new niece."

"What's her name?" Hannah peered over his arm to get a look at her.

"Erica," both Kimberly and Andrew said.

"Give her the baby, Andy." Kimberly ordered.

Hannah blustered, "No, no, that's all right." But Andrew had already extended his arms. Hannah took the infant in her hands, grasping it along its torso, its feet dangling, as though it were a piece of dripping wet laundry. Andrew's eyes twinkled with amusement as he watched.

Kimberly chortled. "It's a baby, not a time bomb!" She thrust the leash back to Andrew, then took the baby from Hannah who was clearly relieved. "Nice to meet you, Hannah. We'll have to get together soon."

"Yes, that would be fun." Hannah replied before the Plat family walked away.

Face to face, Andrew and Hannah stared into each other's eyes, no words needing to be spoken between them. Hannah knew that Andrew knew how particularly important this day was to her. And she knew he had orchestrated the introduction of his sister. She also knew of the pressure both Kimberly and Andrew had put on Bryan to make that apology. It might not be an entirely heartfelt apology, but it was a start.

BID TO LOVE

The breeze blew through Andrew's hair, lifting the short tendrils and messing them up. Her fingers ached to run themselves through the tousled mess, to feel the satiny texture and straighten out the disarray. "Congratulations, Hannah," he said, at last, before dropping a kiss on her cheek.

"Will you and Maggie Mae be able to meet us at the dog park at our usual time?"

"I should be able to break away by then. I'll let you know." Hannah said, her lips pursed as she stood up. It would take a lot to keep her from meeting up with Andrew and he knew it.

"Gosh, I almost forgot to tell you. Miss Rose, an elderly woman here in town has given a huge chunk of money specifically to build the addition on to the shelter I have been wanting." His face beamed with delight, eyes twinkling and his smile ear to ear.

Grasping his hand, Hannah shook it. "Congratulations! That's great news." Her heart hummed with the pleasure she saw on his face.

A vet tech called out to Hannah from the door of the clinic.

"Be right there." Hannah called back.

"Hannah," Andrew said, as she started to walk to the clinic door.

"Yes." Hannah spun around to look at him again, her hair lifting in the breeze.

Andrew swallowed; his eyes fixed on her hair. Then he took her hand and stroked the back of it gently. "Congratulations, again. I can't wait to celebrate later," he said, his eyes flashing with mischief.

"I know I'm springing this on you, and I know you probably aren't expecting it, but I have to tell you how I feel and how much I want you in my life. We've been working together now for nearly half a year. With our work together at the shelter, we've been getting along great, and I think we could make a wonderful team."

Hannah's eyes opened wide, her mouth open but no words coming out, as her heart raced.

He took her hands in his, and staring deeply into her eyes, he whispered, "This isn't a proposal. Not yet anyway. But I think we're heading down that path. And I hope you're willing to walk it with me."

Finding her voice again, as her heart continued to pound with love, "I'm looking forward to it." She kissed his cheek before turning back around and entering the clinic, ready to change her shoes, put on her white coat and do one last check of yesterday's surgery patients before leaving with Andrew.

The End
(for now)

Other books by Diana Rock

<u>Fulton River Falls Series:</u>
Melt My Heart
Proof of Love
Bloomin' In Love
First Christmas Ornament
(release date November 2022)
<u>Colby County Series:</u>
Bid to Love
Courting Choices
<u>MovieStuds Series</u>
Hollywood Hotshot
Hollywood Hotdog (Releases 2023)

Acknowledgements

The following individuals provided much needed help in writing this novel. While I did consult them for their wisdom and experience, any and all mistakes and/or mis-represented material you might find in this book are all my fault, not theirs.

First, I must thank Chris at the Mansfield Animal Control for answering my questions about procedures, equipment, etc.

Second, a special thank you to Officer Rachel Levy with the UCONN Health Center Police Department for answering my questions about charging someone who leaves a dog in a hot car.

Third thank you goes to Dr. Sandra Bushmich, DVM for explaining the euthanasia procedures for animals.

A huge thank you to Dr. Dennis Thibeault, DVM for reading select portions of this manuscript for veterinary practice accuracy. And a special thanks to his daughter for checking it over too!

Special thanks to my beta readers, Patti and Marion for your comments and suggestions. You ladies are the best!

I cannot forget my editor, Lynne Pearson of AllThatEditing.com who slaved over this manuscript early last year before I ripped it to shreds and cut 10K words. Whatever errors may be found entered after her diligent work on this novel are entirely mine.

I cannot forget Desmond's Army Animal Law Advocates (DAALA), who volunteer their time and efforts to speaking for the voiceless animals. They attend every animal abuse court case in Connecticut as well as providing other services to animal victims of abuse, including pledging monetary rewards for information that leads to the arrest and prosecution of animal abusers. A portion of the sales of this book will be donated to DAALA. For more information on this esteemed group, see desmondsarmy.org

BID TO LOVE

Courting Choices
Colby County Series: Book Two

Cortland Stewart smelled like a cow barn. That is to say, cow poop. She sniffed, *Is that a hint of blood.?* The heifer's labor had been long exhausting and messy. But now mother and calf were doing fine. And Cortland, who had been away from her job at Colby County Veterinary Clinic for the entire six-hour labor episode was tired. And hungry.

The call had come in just after five in the morning. Being on large animal duty this week, she had to leave the warmth of her bed to help the mother who was having difficulty birthing her first calf. Breakfast had been a stale bagel without any condiments, while driving to the Sunflower Dairy Farm on the far side of Colby. It was even too early for the local fast-food restaurants to be open.

Her stomach ached and growled as she parked her car alongside the road near the truck stop where lunch wagons and hot dog stands set up every morning to serve the hungry truckers and anyone else who desired a quick take-out meal. Being nearly noon, the place was packed with luncheon traffic.

Five wagons sat in a row that started with a sidewalk style hot dog stand. She sat in the car, gazing at the options: Barbecue, Middle Eastern, Fish & chips, Mexican and Greek. *One of everything please!* As she recalled, the last time she'd been here, she'd had the Fish and chips. Barbecue was too messy, as were the falafel and Tacos. "I guess it's Greek today."

She stepped up to the line, waiting her turn to order. When her nose caught a whiff of the food, her stomach growled so loud the man in front of her turned around and stared with eyes wide open.

"I guess you're hungry, little lady." He duffed his baseball cap and with cavalier-style, wave her to step before him.

Her face burning, Cortland held up her palm. "No, that's quite all right. I can wait."

He nodded his head and replaced his hat. "Suit yourself." Before turning around, the man sniffed. "Is that you?" He asked, his face scrunched up in disgust.

Her body tensed, drawing itself into a tighter, more compact form, as if that might stop or mitigate the vile odor coming from her clothes and person. With a sigh, she promised herself to complain to Barbra that the disposable Tyvek coveralls for just such a purpose were completely useless. "I'm sorry, yes. I spent the morning in a cow barn. I apologize for the smell."

He duffed his hat again to scratch his forehead. "Cow barn? What were you doing there? Milking?"

Not wanting to get into too much detail about her morning, Cortland shook her head and only said, "Helping a calf come into the world."

"Yikes, no wonder you stink." He turned back around and stepped forward as the line had moved up.

Rolling her eyes, Cortland pulled out her cell phone and called the clinic. It was about time she let them know where she was and when she would be back in the building.

The receptionist, Alissa answered. "Colby County Veterinary Clinic, how may I help you?"

"Hey, It's me, Cortland. I'll be there in about twenty minutes. I'm just grabbing a bit to eat, I'm starving."

"No problem. Your next client isn't until one o'clock."

Cortland felt her anxiety level drop several notches. "Great. What is it?"

"A guinea pig. Not acting normal."

"Greaaaat. No rest for this wicked woman."

"You and me both." And the call ended.

Noticing she was up next to order, she scanned the chalkboard menu looking for her favorite.

Stepping up the truck window, she called out, "Hey Nick, How are you today?"

"Better than you from the looks of it." He picked up his pencil and scrawled on an order pad. "What you having, love?"

"Chicken souvlaki, no fries. Please. And a diet Dr. Pepper."

"You got it."

She paid for the meal, accepting her can of soda from Nick before stepping aside to wait in the cluster of people at the pick-up window.

It was another five minutes before George, Nick's brother called out "chicken souvlaki". Without thinking, Cortland stepped forward, reaching for the Styrofoam takeout container. Grasping the left side of the container, she was surprised to find the right side of the container was gripped by a large, dirty, masculine hand.

Dumbfounded by the action she looked at the hand's owner. Tall, dark, and probably handsome underneath all that black soot and dirt. His face was rugged beneath all that grime, his scruffy chin rather squared off. But his teal-blue eyes blazed through under thick eyebrows,

"That's mine." His jaw hardened as she would not let go of the container.

"I think it's mine. I ordered the chicken souvlaki." As the breeze shifted she caught a whiff of him. Smoke. He stunk of smoke. Glancing down his length, she saw a light brown tee shirt stained with large areas of sweat and black along the edges of his short sleeves and hem.

"So did I. I called ahead ten minutes ago." He continued, his tight grip on the Styrofoam starting to crush the container. "I'm in a hurry."

"You stink worse than me." She pulled on the Styrofoam, but he held on. "I have a client to meet in an hour. And I have to shower and change beforehand." Really, the last thing she wanted was a tug-of-war with a man over her lunch order.

"I have to return to the firehouse, asap." Turning toward the order window he called out, "Hey Nick, is this one mine or hers?"

DIANA ROCK

About the Author

Diana Rock lives in eastern Connecticut with her tall, dark, and handsome hero and one elderly diva cat.

A Histotechnologists by day, she writes at night.

For fun, she cooks, bakes, hikes, gardens, and fly fishes. She also loves to go dancing with the New Haven Chapter of the Royal Scottish Country Dance Society.

Don't miss out!

Visit the website below and you can sign up to receive emails whenever Diana Rock publishes a new book. There's no charge and no obligation.

https://books2read.com/r/B-A-YUKN-BRNUB

BOOKS 2 READ

Connecting independent readers to independent writers.

About the Author

Diana lives in eastern Connecticut with her tall, dark and handsome hero and one spoiled elderly kitty. She works full time as a histotechnologist, writing in her spare time. Diana likes puttering about the yard, baking and cooking, hiking, fly-fishing, and Scottish Country Dancing. Follow her exploits on her website, in her blogs and newsletters.

Read more at DianaRock.com.

CPSIA information can be obtained
at www.ICGtesting.com
Printed in the USA
BVHW040551040922
646102BV00003B/14